CHILD X

CHILD
X

Lee Weatherly

David Fickling Books

OXFORD · NEW YORK

A DAVID FICKLING BOOK

Published by David Fickling Books
an imprint of Random House Children's Books
a division of Random House, Inc.
1540 Broadway
New York, New York 10036

Published simultaneously in Canada by Random House of Canada Limited,
Toronto, and in Great Britain by David Fickling Books, a division of
Random House Children's Books

www.randomhouse.com/teens

Library of Congress Cataloging-in-Publication Data
Weatherly, Lee.
Child X / Lee Weatherly.
p. ; cm.
Summary: Thirteen-year-old Jules finds her predictable and, except for the
friction between her parents, not unpleasant life completely turned upside
down when her beloved father suddenly leaves home, refuses to speak to her,
and reporters begin hounding her everywhere she goes.
ISBN 0-385-75009-9
[1. Family problems—Fiction. 2. Theater—Fiction.
3. Fathers and daughters—Fiction. 4. Identity—Fiction.] I. Title
PZ7.W3553 Ch 2002
[Fic]—dc21
2002020667

Printed in the United States of America

June 2002

10 9 8 7 6 5 4 3 2 1

First American Edition

Special thanks to Philip Pullman for graciously allowing the use of character names and situations from his novel *Northern Lights*.

Thanks also to:

The Hurst County Secondary School, Tadley

Clare Sager, for offering her time and comments

And Liz Kessler, for providing just the right input at just the right time. Thanks, EFF!

*For my parents, who gave me books
and cheered my writing from the start.
Thanks and love.*

Note to American Readers:

Philip Pullman's novel *Northern Lights* was published in the United States as *The Golden Compass.*

The mention of SATS refers not to the American SAT's, but to assessment tests given to students in Great Britain in Year Nine (ninth grade).

Chapter One

Janet Griegson passed me a scrap of newspaper today in maths, all folded over like a note. From Marty, of course, my best friend. She sits on the other side of Janet, ever since Miss Chatworth separated us for whispering too much. Now I'm at a table all by myself, like a leper.

Marty leaned across her desk to look at me, motioning like wild. *Read it!* she mouthed. So I unfolded the bit of newspaper, and saw this:

> **The Flying Frog Theatre's spring production promises to be as much fun as always. Children aged seven to sixteen are invited to audition for *Northern Lights*, adapted for the stage from the popular children's book by Philip Pullman. Auditions Friday from 4 pm to 10 pm. Come one, come all!**

And I'm not being funny, but I swear I got tingles. *Destiny!* I've always wanted to be an actress, always. Dad says I was acting before I even learned to talk – pulling faces just to make people laugh, putting on funny costumes and different personalities like other people put on hats.

I stared down at the article. *Northern Lights* is my favourite book ever, in the whole world. And Lyra, in that spooky alternate Oxford, is my favourite heroine.

I could be Lyra.

Two rows across, Marty was bent over her exercise book doing equations like she actually cared about them. When she got the chance, she craned her neck to look at me, and raised her eyebrows up so that they almost disappeared under her curly dark hair. Are you game? And I grinned back. Yes!

Marty is Martine really, but everyone calls her Marty. Like I'm Jules, even though I'm Juliet. Only teachers and my grandmother ever call me Juliet, which is an OK name if you're a Shakespearean maiden waiting for your true love on a balcony, but in real life? Way too posh and prissy. Nothing at all like me.

The bell went then. The whole class jumped and started rustling about, shoving books and pencil cases into their bookbags.

'Stop!' bellowed Chatty. 'Military fashion! Do *not* move until I tell you so!'

Oh, please. She made us stand by our desks, twitching and itching to leave, until she finally *condescended* to release us. Then – whoosh! Everyone gone at once, scattered in different directions.

Marty and I rushed towards the science building, shivering. It's January, and grey and freezing outside.

'Doesn't the play sound *great*?' said Marty, huddling into her blazer. 'It'd be so cool if we both got parts!'

'I know! The only plays I've ever been in are those incredibly sad things in primary school.'

Marty nodded. 'Everyone being spring flowers or whatever.'

'Twinkly little elves. Exactly.'

'Will your dad drive us to the audition?'

My dad works from home, and he never minds driving us to things. (He's a writer for the BBC.) So I said 'Sure,' automatically, and then I said, 'No, wait, let's get the bus, all right? I don't want to ask him this time.'

'Wha-at? Why not, you moron?' Marty bumped me with her hip.

I bumped her back. ' 'Cause I want to surprise him if I get a part.'

This isn't like a proper book so far, is it? I should tell you something about myself, what I look like and all. So I'll start again.

My name is Jules Cheney, and I'm thirteen. And if you haven't guessed already, I have to tell you I'm practically the queen of Year Nine – I have long red hair and a million best friends and I'm so popular you'd just about *die* if I sat next to you or ate lunch with you or—

Sorry, I can't go on, I'm laughing too hard. I've got long red hair, all right. But you probably wouldn't notice me at all, really. Unless you saw me and Marty carrying on together, laughing and whispering like we always do.

But with most people I'm sort of shy. Or not *shy*, exactly, just quiet. Unless I know you really well. Then Dad says you can't shut me up unless you gag me. But most people don't know me really well, and so a lot of times when I'm called on in class, my mind goes an utter blank, and I get all red and flustered. It's very embarrassing. Adrian Benton calls me Brickface when that happens, and then everyone laughs and my face blazes even redder.

Not that I care what Adrian Benton says. Or does. No-one likes him. He has this horrible braying laugh and he's always bouncing about like a chubby, hyper puppy, trying to make everyone notice him. Pathetic.

I helped Dad get tea ready that night like I usually do. I grated up cheese while he chopped onions, and in the background the little kitchen CD-player was pulsing out this weird music called Enigma that Dad likes.

'I'll be home late on Friday,' I told him. 'Only it's a secret why, OK?'

Dad shook his head and laughed. 'Anything I want to know about?'

'Not really. Just murder and mayhem.' That's what I always say.

'Thought as much.' Dad pointed his knife at me. 'I

don't know you if the coppers come. And home by six, right?'

'Um – I don't know if I will be.'

He lifted his eyebrows, and I said, 'Mrs Fulson knows where we'll be.' That's Marty's mum. 'She said she'd drive us home afterwards. It's nothing bad, just a surprise.'

At least, I hope there's a surprise. You see, *Northern Lights* is Dad's favourite book, too. When I first got it, we read it out loud to each other. (It took ages – it's a stonking great book.) It would be brilliant if I could tell him I'd got a part! He'd be so, so chuffed.

Now he just smiled and said, 'Ve-ry mysterious . . . ring me if you're going to be later than six, then, and tell me what time you plan on swanning home. I presume they have phones in this secret place?'

'Well, of course,' I said. Do theatres have phones? I don't know, I hope so. I'd have to remember to take twenty pence with me.

We had just popped Dad's special mash in the oven for the cheddar to melt when the phone rang.

Dad answered it, motioning for me to turn down the music. 'Hello?' There was a pause, and then his face turned grim. 'Again? Holly, come on, you said you'd be home on time for a change.'

My stomach sank. Mum home late again. That meant another fight.

'There's *always* a meeting. Yes, fair enough, but meanwhile I've got tea just about ready, because you *told* me that tonight, for once, you were not going to be late.'

Another pause. Dad grimaced, glaring at the oven. Finally he said, 'Whatever. Fine. See you then.' He put the phone down with a bang. 'Well, it's just me and thee. Again.'

I put on a really happy face. 'Great! I'll get the plates.' I hummed as I set the table, larking about and pretending to tap-dance and in general acting like everything was wonderful, hoping that maybe Dad would relax a bit and forget about being mad at Mum.

It didn't work. He scowled all the way through tea. Then he scowled all the way through pud. It got really late, past eight o'clock. We were both watching the clock and pretending not to, while my stomach got tighter and tighter. I *hate* it, *hate* it when they fight. Though you'd think I'd be used to it by now. *Why* can't Mum ever be home on time?

We had almost finished doing the dishes when the key rattled in the lock. Dad threw the sponge down on the counter and slammed out of the kitchen. I kept on drying, slowly. Wipe, wipe. Listen, listen.

Mutters and mumbles from the front room, with an occasional phrase bursting through.

Dad: 'Fine, don't come home, but you could at least . . .'

Mum: 'Well, what I was supposed to do? I was on a conference call from Brussels, I couldn't just . . .'

And so on. And on. They only have this argument about three nights a week. The rest of the time they go for a bit of pot luck, and fight about whatever's handy.

By the time I finished drying the last dish, the TV was on and I couldn't hear them anymore. I edged open the kitchen door. Mum was curled up on the settee with her shoes off, watching TV, and Dad was sitting at the dining table, typing on his laptop. Phew. Battle over.

Mum looked dead tired, but her face lit up when she saw me. 'Hi, sweetie. Nice day at school?'

'OK.' I ran and jumped onto the settee on my knees, jostling her up and down, and she laughed. 'Oi, Mighty Mouse, stop it.'

'*You're* Mighty Mouse, not me.' I bounced even harder. We're both Mighty Mouse, because Mum's really tiny, like me, only she has short black hair. We have the same eyes, too – dark brown with little green flecks.

She's an international financier. I'm not sure what that is, only it sounds incredibly boring. But she gets very excited about it. She'll be going on about Tokyo and the yen and all that, and I'll be sitting there with my eyes glazed, trying not to pass out. I think Dad is too, actually, but when they're not arguing, he'll nod and say things like, Really? That must be difficult for you, and Wow, well done.

They're pretty much opposites anyway. Dad's tall and thin, with curly brown hair and green eyes. He slopes around in jeans, and wears a leather jacket and rides a motorcycle, and then you have Mum with her business suits and Prada shoes and Dior perfume. Occasionally, Dad has to spiff up for some BBC do or other, and then they look like they actually belong together.

Which is a relief. They don't usually seem like they belong together at all.

'Quit messing around, Jules, you've got home-work,' Dad called over now.

Groan. I got out my books and dumped them on the dining table. Dad moved some of his notes and his laptop out of my way, and stood up to stretch.

'What about tomorrow night?' he said suddenly to Mum. 'Are you going to be home *then*?'

Oh, God. It wasn't over after all.

Mum looked up, surprised. She turned down the volume on the remote. 'Tomorrow night – oh, right, Sophie's birthday. Thursday, let me think—'

'You forgot all about it, didn't you? It's only been arranged for *weeks* now, Holly.'

'No, no. It won't be a problem. I'll be there. It's all arranged, it's in my diary. I'm sure it is.'

Dad looked at her for a second, like – yeah, right. But he didn't say anything. Instead, he plucked a couple of satsumas from the crystal bowl on the piano. 'Jules, heads up.' He tossed one to me from behind his back. I had to lean way over to catch it.

'How old will Granny Sophie be?' I dropped satsuma rinds on my maths homework, all over the horrid equations. Take that, Chatty.

'Sixty-one,' said Dad. 'Be ready to blow out a *lot* of candles.'

'Really, Ben, you'll set the house on fire,' murmured Mum. She turned the volume back up.

'Is Uncle Derek coming?' I asked.

Dad rolled his eyes and didn't answer. I knew that probably meant yes.

Chapter Two

It did, too. The next night, I heard Uncle Derek's laugh all over the house the minute he and Gran walked in, and then a second later he was in the kitchen and had scooped me up, swinging me around. 'Juliet, Juliet! Wherefore are thou, Juliet?'

Uncle Derek is like a big red-headed cyclone. He's loads of fun, but I hardly ever get to see him. Actually, I probably see him on TV more than I do in real life. He's an actor. He's been in loads of films and TV shows and stuff. (Dad says he's bigger than life, or at least his head is.)

He was still swinging me about. ' "Wherefore art thou" is *Juliet's* line,' I giggled.

'Ah! Then that must be the east,' (he pointed to Dad) 'and you, fair Juliet, are the sun!'

Granny Sophie appeared in the kitchen door, wearing one of her smart black suits and dripping with gold jewellery. She always looks like she should be Mum's mum instead of Dad's. 'Hello, darlings.' She gave Dad and me pecks on the cheek.

I saw Dad frown at the clock. Six thirty-four. My

stomach jerked. Oh, Mum, *please* don't be late again!

'Doesn't she look splendid, our old mum?' Uncle Derek put an arm around Granny Sophie and shook her a bit. 'You'd never know she was over the hill, would you?' She gave him a withering look, but you could see she was trying not to smile.

'You're incorrigible. Ben, that roast smells lovely.'

'If it doesn't burn before Holly gets here,' said Dad.

'It'd be *nice* burnt!' I put in quickly. 'We could have it, what do you call it, *chargrilled*. People pay loads of money to have their food chargrilled, don't they? It's dead trendy.' I stuck my nose up in the air and peered haughtily at him over invisible spectacles. Laugh, Dad!

Uncle Derek laughed, all right. He offered me his arm and we minced about the kitchen together, being too too posh.

'I quite *fancy* a bit of chargrilled peasant tonight, don't you, Lady Horseface?'

'Oh, indubitably, Sir Twaddle!'

Even Granny Sophie smiled. Dad just said, 'Hmm,' and looked at the roast. Which isn't at all like him, really it isn't. Usually he's the best laugh in the world. Except for lately.

Lately, he and Mum haven't been laughing much at all.

Finally Uncle Derek dropped my arm and leaned against the fridge, watching Dad cook. 'So . . . how's life at the Beeb?'

Dad didn't look up from chopping mushrooms.

'Great. They've just renewed my contract for another series. Four scripts, all at their top rate.' Then he did look up, and smiled a sharp-eyed smile.

Here they go again. I think it's sort of funny, but I saw Granny Sophie sigh and press her lips together.

'Well, that must have been a nice surprise for you.' Uncle Derek stroked his bushy red beard, which he grew for the TV show he's in now. It's called *Sole Survivor*. He plays an angst-ridden deep-sea fisherman. 'Did I tell you we've just started taping the second series of *my* show?'

'You did, actually.'

'Publicity's coming along a treat. We might have someone famous in the family before much longer.'

Dad ripped a head of broccoli to bits. 'Great,' he said tightly. 'Can't complain either, I suppose. Ian says one of the episodes I wrote last series has been tipped for a Golden TV award.'

'Oh, well done.' Pause. 'Did I tell you about the spread they're planning on me in *Entertainment Magazine?*'

Honestly, it's like they're six years old sometimes. You've got an Action Man? Ha! I've got *two* Action Men *and* a super-powered transmogrifier!

The front door slammed. Mum rushed into the kitchen, still wearing her coat and looking breathless. 'Sorry, I—'

Dad kissed her on the cheek. 'Better late than never, hmm, my sweet?' he purred.

Mum flushed. 'You said quarter past or *half six*. It's only just gone half six now.'

Granny and Uncle Derek sprang into action. Lovely to see you Holly darling, kiss kiss, hug hug. Braver than me! I wouldn't have got between the pair of them without a bullet-proof vest.

Mum's mouth was still stiff when they let go of her. 'How about some wine?' she said, opening the fridge. She took out a bottle of white wine and attacked it with a corkscrew.

'Here, let me, love. You're mangling it.' Uncle Derek took it away from her and started peeling off the metal bit around the top. It curled away in a thin strip.

'I was actually going to open a *red*, to go with the roast,' said Dad.

'Well, this will be the starter, then, won't it?' snapped Mum. She left the kitchen, pulling off her coat.

Uncle Derek looked at us enquiringly, holding the corkscrew. Dad waved a hand at him.

'Oh, go on, now you've started. Have it in the dining room, why don't you? Let me cook in peace.' He smiled as he said it, but he didn't look hugely thrilled.

Uncle Derek snorted. 'Genius at work, eh?'

'Some of us actually *do* work.'

'Some of us are incredible drama queens.' Uncle Derek flung a hand to his brow. 'Leave me to cook in peace – no, no, just leave me, I'll survive somehow—'

'Oh, that's rich, coming from *you*—'

'Not on my birthday, please.' Granny Sophie patted Dad on the shoulder, and she and Uncle Derek headed out of the kitchen. I started to follow.

'Not you, Jules,' said Dad. A bit shortly, I thought.

And I guess he thought so, too, because then he shook his head and grinned at me. 'Sorry. I could use some help, OK?'

He took the roast out (which smelled totally yum and didn't look the least bit burnt) and started making gravy. 'Tell me about your day,' he said. 'What's the latest instalment in the fascinating life of Jules Cheney?'

I measured out the frozen peas. 'Fascinating, right.'

'Fascinating to *me*. Come on, talk.'

So I told him what we were doing at school, which was mostly one boring SATS study sheet after another, with some Tudors thrown in. And what Marty and I had talked about at lunch, only I didn't tell him *all* of that, because mostly we had talked about the audition tomorrow – chills, fear! But I did tell him how Marty keeps droning on about this boy in our form called David Tallis.

'Got a crush, eh?' Dad poured the gravy in a serving dish.

'More like a *crash*. It's really, really boring. She keeps asking me if I think he likes her. Like, twelve times a day.'

Dad laughed. 'You just wait. That'll be you, sooner than you think.'

Yeah, right! OK, maybe some of the Year Elevens are pretty gorgeous, but believe me, the boys in our year are *not* anything to drool over. (Adrian Benton springs to mind as a classic example.)

Dad put the roast on a serving plate. 'We have ignition!' He handed me a bowl of peas and another one of roast potatoes. I took them through and sat down at the dining table with the others.

Uncle Derek was pouring Mum and Granny Sophie more wine. 'Where's *your* glass, Jules? My word, your dad isn't raising you right, is he? Go and tell him you want some wine and you want it now.'

I stuck my tongue out at him, and Mum laughed. Then Dad came in with the roast, and she stopped smiling like someone had flipped a switch.

'Ooh, lovely,' said Granny Sophie.

Uncle Derek put the bottle down and winked at me. 'I should fritter about writing all day, too. Your domestic skills are coming along a treat, Ben.'

'Ha ha,' said Dad. He started carving the roast. 'Not much chance of you working without an audience to admire you though, is there?' He looked up and smiled when he said it, like he was joking, and Uncle Derek raised an eyebrow and smiled back.

Then Dad sat down and poured everyone *red* wine, except for me – I got sparkling water, which I love. We toasted Granny Sophie again, and settled down to eat.

Granny Sophie cut all of her food into tiny pieces, her fork and knife going clink, clink, clink, while she shot questions at me.

'How are you doing in school?'

'Um . . . OK, I guess.'

'Do you like maths?'

'Well – not *really*. I mean—'

'Very important, maths. You must do well at it to get ahead, believe me. And what about homework? How much homework are they giving you?'

Granny Sophie used to scare me when I was younger. Well, maybe she still does, a tiny bit. She stares at you while you talk, with these dark, intense, *probing* eyes. Question after question, then stare, stare, until after a while I got so nervous I dropped my fork. It clattered against the plate and my cheeks flared up. Argh! Like they always do!

Dad jumped in then with, 'Jules is doing really well this term, Mum. She's been working hard.' Which isn't really true, but it was nice of him to say.

Uncle Derek laughed. 'Oh, who cares how she does in *school*, anyway? There are more important things in life.' He poured himself more wine, sloshing little red drops on to the tablecloth.

Dad gave him a narrow look. 'Like what?'

'Like art. Life! Jules is going to be an *actress*, aren't you, my darling?'

My face blazed even redder, and I wanted to sink into the floor. *How* could he put me on the spot like that?

'Even if she becomes an actress—'

'*If?* She's an actress already! It's in her blood, like the curse of the Cheney red hair.'

Granny Sophie said, 'Yes, Juliet's hair is just like my mother's. And of course your uncle Stanley has the hair as well. It's so funny; once in every generation, it seems to—'

'Mum, we know all that,' interrupted Dad. He was still frowning at Uncle Derek. 'The point is that Juliet needs a good education.'

Uncle Derek snorted. 'Well, of course she does – in

theatre. What she needs is good drama tuition some-where, not to be wasting her time memorizing the Battle of Hastings and that rubbish. Who cares? You can look it up in a book.'

'Thank you for that extremely mature point of view,' said Dad. 'And when *you* have children, you can warp them all you like, but I would actually prefer that my daughter be slightly better rounded than you, if you don't mind. She's in one of the best-rated schools in Surrey, and—'

'Oh, you just know all the answers, don't you?' said Mum suddenly. She had been sitting quietly, sipping her wine. Now she put her glass down with a sharp *click*. 'You're so controlling. Why don't you just ask Jules what she'd like to do?'

No, don't, leave me out of it! My throat tightened up. I kept eating, chewing merrily away like nothing was wrong.

Dad glared at Mum, his eyes like glinting green marbles. 'Keep out of this, all right? What do *you* know about what she needs?'

Granny Sophie cleared her throat. 'Whatever Juliet decides to do will be fine, I'm sure. May I have some more vegetables, please?'

Uncle Derek passed them to her silently. Mum stared at Dad, white-faced. 'I do think I know my own child.'

'How? You're never *here*.'

'I'm still her *mother*, thank you very much!'

'Yes, and I'm the one who takes care of her, aren't I? Her *father*.'

Words spat out of Mum's mouth: 'Oh, you may take *care* of her, but—' She stopped abruptly, looking as startled as if she had spoken in Swahili. She glanced at Uncle Derek, then down at her plate. A flush crept over her neck.

'What?' said Dad.

'Nothing.'

'What were you going to say?'

'*Nothing!*'

They kept on like this for a few minutes. Then Mum threw her napkin down and left the table, with Dad following her. Their voices drifted out from the kitchen, low and hissing.

I stared down at my plate, trying not to cry. Why can't they go one *single solitary* night without shouting at each other? And why did it have to be over *me* this time?

A hand touched my shoulder. Uncle Derek. I looked at him and he sort of smiled, raising his glass. 'Never mind, love. Here, have some plonk.' And he poured a big dollop of wine into my sparkling water.

It wasn't very nice.

Granny Sophie and Uncle Derek left soon after that, calling a taxi to carry them off into the night. Lucky them.

Normally I'd have helped with the washing-up, but there was no way I was going into that kitchen. I'd sooner shove my hand in a wasps' nest. So I went to bed instead, and lay awake for ages, thinking about the audition the next day. I even got out my copy of

Northern Lights and started reading through it, looking for Lyra's speeches and planning how I'd say them.

In no time at all I got so caught up in the story that I forgot why I was even looking at it. I've read it six times already, but it gets better every time. Lyra, who's so gutsy and brave (and so *not* like me) and that incredible world she lives in, just a shadow or so away from ours, where everyone has their own personal daemon! I'd give anything if that were real. I'd have a snowy white cat, with silky long hair and amber eyes.

When it was almost eleven o'clock, I went out onto the landing to try and hear if they were still at it or not. Except I didn't have to *try* to hear at all. They had got louder than ever, really screaming at each other.

'*You have to tell me the truth!*' shouted Dad. *Crash!* I flinched. It sounded like he had thrown a pile of pots and pans onto the floor.

'Don't you dare threaten me!' Mum screamed back.

I stood there gripping the landing railing, trying not to shake. Dad, throwing things?

I turned and dashed back down the corridor into my room, shutting the door and practically diving under the duvet, hiding in a little cave. I couldn't hear them anymore, but they were still down there, saying horrible things . . . oh, *please* stop! Were they still arguing about me? No, it sounded like Mum was lying about something – tell Dad the truth about *what*?

It was a very long time before I got to sleep.

Chapter Three

I woke up the next morning at half seven, just before the alarm went off. Were they still fighting? My stomach clenched. I put on my grey school trousers and burgundy jumper, tied my hair back in a pony-tail, and tiptoed downstairs.

Mum was in the dining room, dressed for work and drinking a cup of coffee. The dishes from the night before were all cleared away. Everything looked peaceful and normal. Except that Mum's eyes were red, and her smile looked like a stretched rubber band. 'Good morning, sweetie. Have some breakfast.'

So I had some cereal I didn't want, and sat there trying to think of something to say. Well, actually, I could think of quite a bit to say – like, what were you lying to Dad about, and do the pair of you still want to rip each other's throats out? Do you suppose Granny Sophie had a nice birthday dinner? Why can't you ever, *ever* come home on time, so that the two of you don't fight so much?

I could hardly swallow, the air felt so soggy and heavy.

Finally, Mum cleared her throat. 'I'll be driving you to school this morning. Your dad's still asleep.'

'You don't need to drive me. I always walk.' *How* can you just sit there casually slurping coffee?

'I'll drive you anyway. It's on my way to the station.'

That's all we said to each other. I slammed the car door as Mum dropped me off at school.

'What did you bring to wear?' asked Marty at lunch.

I swallowed a bite of chicken pie. 'My blue jumper.'

'The one with the stripe?'

'No, the dark blue one. And some jeans.'

Marty nodded. 'Cool. I brought my black trousers. And my black top with the sort of glittery stars on it.'

My bite of pie stuck in my throat. Oh no! Should I have brought dressier clothes? Because Marty looked *amazingly* sexy and mature in that top. And even though I didn't think sexy and mature were really what Lyra was supposed to look like, I still felt a pretty serious pang. No-one would look twice at me with Marty around.

A burst of laughter from behind us. We twisted round in our seats and saw Vicki Young and her crowd, standing around Janet Griegson, who was clutching her lunch tray to her chest like a shield.

'Can you smell it?' asked Vicki. They all sniffed.

'Yup,' said Georgina, pretending to gag.

Janet looked around, trying to be casual and ignore them, but her eyes were bright. Every time she tried to walk away, one of Vicki's gang moved in front of her, blocking her in.

'Phew!' Anne Faroni waved her hand in front of her. 'She *reeks!*'

Vicki shook her head sorrowfully. 'Don't you ever *wash* after you go to the stables, Janet? Don't you *care* if you pong like a pony?'

'Pony pong!' shrieked Georgina. 'What a great name for her!'

Finally Janet got away from them, and sat at the end of our table, staring down at her chicken pie and chips.

Marty leaned over to her. 'Vicki's got even worse this term, hasn't she? I don't know why the teachers don't *do* something about her.'

'It's true, she's really horrible,' I added.

Janet nodded, wiping her eyes. Vicki and that lot used to spend their time picking on Adrian, who admittedly deserved it. But I suppose they got bored, since he just leapt about and laughed at everything they said. Still, at least he did *something*. Better than Janet, who just sat there being sodden.

Vicki walked past smirking, her perfect blonde hair swinging from side to side. 'Doesn't the *odour* bother you, Jules?'

And even though smarting off to Vicki is *not* a good idea, suddenly I heard myself say, 'Yeah, it does. You should try taking a shower or something, Vicki.'

Her face reddened as the table behind us started whooping with laughter. 'Watch it, *midget*,' she hissed.

The Flying Frog Theatre is run by adults, of course, but all the acting is done by kids. Marty and I rushed in around five o'clock that afternoon to find about three hundred of them running around and jumping about and ignoring their parents bleating at them to behave, and in general behaving totally immaturely. We stood to one side to make it *very* clear that we had nothing to do with them.

'Um . . . where do we go?' Marty's eyes widened as she looked around the empty theatre. I mean, full of kids, but empty of an audience. It did look strange to see the stage with its red curtains gaping open and no scenery, just bare boards and a blank concrete wall at the back.

A great ball of butterflies rustled about in my stomach as I stared at it. *Anything at all* could happen in that stark place. And I can't explain it, but it just felt like home, instantly. I could hardly wait to get up on that stage!

We took off our coats. 'How do I look?' asked Marty.

'Great. Me?'

'Great. Are you sure you don't want any eyeshadow?'

'Yes . . . are you *sure* I look OK?'

'You look great.' Marty looked at herself in a little compact, then snapped it shut and put it in her bag.

We had changed into our normal clothes before we left school, and played around with putting on blue sparkly eyeshadow and lipstick. Only, I ended up putting some on and then wiping it all off again. I *hate* being so small sometimes! I looked like a ten-year-old playing at dressing-up. Marty looked about sixteen.

A frazzled-looking lady with flyaway brown hair swooped down on us, clutching a clipboard. 'Are you here to audition, dears?' She took our names, and then said, '121 and 122,' and slapped numbered sticky labels on us. Right on the front of my jumper, thanks very much!

She herded us to the biggest group of kids, over at the side of the stage. All girls. Every shape, size and colour you could imagine. Marty clutched my arm. 'I bet they all want to be Lyra!' Which made the butterflies in my stomach go mad with twitching about.

'Number 82,' called a woman sitting out in the middle of all the empty seats.

I poked Marty. 'That'll be the director,' I whispered, showing off a bit. Uncle Derek's taken me along to tapings a few times.

The frazzled lady shoved sheets of paper in front of us. 'Here's what you have to read. Ignore the first paragraph, just read the second long one.'

'Is there a phone around somewhere?' Marty asked the lady. I was already reading through the sheet, devouring it in big gulps. Lyra, telling John Faa and Farder Coram about her quest. I knew just how I wanted to do it, too – sort of low and fierce and sad.

Marty pulled at my sleeve. 'Jules, come on, we have to phone.' I looked at my watch and it was half five already. So I followed Marty out to the lobby, and after she rang her mum I put in twenty pence to ring Dad.

But Mum answered instead, on the first ring. '*Hello?*'

'Mum? What are you doing home so soon?'

'Oh, well I . . .' her voice sort of trailed off. She cleared her throat. 'Where are you?' So I explained, and made her promise not to tell Dad.

'Have you – have you spoken to your father today?'

She sounded strange, like her voice was too thick for her throat.

'No . . . I've been at *school*, remember? Mum, what's wrong?' My fingers tightened around the receiver.

There was another long pause. Marty stood staring at me, with the lobby so empty and quiet it practically echoed around us.

'Nothing's wrong,' said Mum finally. Her voice sounded normal again. 'Good luck, darling. I'll see you when you get home.'

I hung up.

'Is everything OK?' asked Marty.

'I *think* so . . . they had another fight last night, that's all.' Marty made a sympathetic face and squeezed my arm.

We went back and waited for ages and ages, through number after number. My feet started to hurt. I snuck glances at the girls left standing in our group, trying to picture each of them as Lyra.

Suddenly Marty's hands flew up over her mouth. 'Oh *no*, I don't believe it!' she moaned through her fingers.

I looked up on the stage, and it was Adrian Benton! Ick, puke, blech! *Adrian Benton*, in all his chubby glory, reading out the polar bear's speech in this gratey, growly voice. 'I am a warrior! I do what needs to be done.' Brown hair half-covered his eyes. He shoved it back as he motioned with one hand.

I hate to admit this, but he was really good. So good that I forgot to elbow Marty and snicker at the idea of him being a warrior.

24

When he finished, the director said, 'Very nice. Thank you.' Adrian hopped down the stairs. As he walked past our group, he saw me and grinned his stupid, floppy grin. 'Hey, it's Brickface!'

Of course the hated red whooshed up my cheeks, right on cue. Kill! I would have given *anything* at that moment for the power of blasting him into dust with one deadly flick of my eyes. *Zap, sizzle.* What's that singed mark on the carpet? Oh, that's where Adrian Benton met his doom.

Instead I just glared at him, and almost missed my number being called out.

'That's you!' Marty pushed me.

The stage yawned before me. And when I got to the middle of it and looked out, I could see *everything*. Rows and rows of empty seats, with the director sitting in the middle of them, a woman with lots of freckles and tumbled blonde hair. I could even see the slight furrows on her forehead as we stared at each other.

'You *are* number 121, aren't you? Go on, dear.'

A snicker from off to the side. Adrian, laughing at me! I looked down at my sheet and started reading wildly, almost spitting the words out:

'I thought Mrs Coulter was nice, right, but then I found out she was in charge of the Gobblers! They took my friend Roger. He just disappeared one day, and I never saw him again. And they've got my uncle locked up, too – they've got the armoured bears guarding him, somewhere in the north. I'm going to rescue him, and Roger too. I'll do it or die. . .'

When I finished, there was silence. The director sat

leaning forward, her arms on her knees, nodding slightly. But all she said was, 'Very nice. Thank you. Number 122, please.'

'You were *great*,' Marty told me again. 'You sounded so ferocious! When you said, "I'll do it or die," I really *believed* you.'

'Really? Really really?'

We were standing outside the theatre, waiting for Marty's mum to pick us up, stamping our feet on the pavement to keep warm. Marty nodded, her dark hair curling out from under her hood. 'Really. Everyone around me stopped talking when you read. I heard one girl say, "Why bother trying after that?"'

'You did *not!*'

'I did.'

'Really?'

She nodded. 'And she was right. You'll get called back for sure. You were really *good*. Much better than me. I could hear my voice shaking the whole time I read. I was *terrible*.'

And it's awful to say, but she really *hadn't* been that great. 'Don't be silly, we'll both get parts,' I told her. 'Right?' I nudged her, but she just made a face.

So I waved my hands about in twining patterns, casting a spell: 'I have said it, now let it be done. We'll both . . . get . . . parts!' That's from when we used to play wizards and warlocks.

Marty gave me a sour look. '*You* will, anyway.'

I let my arms fall, and put my hands back in my

pockets. What if I got a part and she didn't? I'd feel terrible, but not anywhere near as terrible as I'd feel if *she* got a part and *I* didn't. I blew out my breath in little white puffs, and pretended to be scanning Whitley Road for their blue Ford Fiesta.

'Bye, Brickface,' shouted a voice. Adrian Benton, getting into a battered white Toyota, waving his ski-cap at us as if he were setting off on a cruise or something. I wish. Ugh! I turned away quickly.

'Adrian was really good as well,' said Marty. She had a funny, pinched smile on her face. 'Maybe you'll get to be in the play together. I think he fancies you, you know.'

Which I thought was *totally* uncalled for.

When I got home, the house felt dead quiet. The television was off, and I could hear the refrigerator humming in the kitchen. Mum sat curled in the corner of the sofa, smoking a cigarette. Her face looked puffy. I dropped my bag on the floor and waited for her to ask me about the audition. Instead, she just looked at me.

'Mum, what is it? Is something wrong?'

She looked away and ground her cigarette out into the bronze ashtray. There were already a dozen crumpled fag-ends there. And she's supposed to be cutting down.

I looked around nervously. The house felt so *quiet*. 'Where's Dad?'

Mum sort of gasped and groped for the box of tissues on the coffee table – and all at once I realized she'd been crying. Panic swooped over me. I grabbed at her arm. '*Mum?* Mum, where's Dad? He's OK, isn't he? Where *is* he?'

She blew her nose with a pink tissue, dabbed at her eyes. 'He's fine. That's not what's wrong. Sit down, Jules.'

I perched beside her, trembling, waiting for the worst.

But I had no idea it was going to be the worst *ever*. The worst *possible*.

Mum cleared her throat, avoiding my eyes. 'Your father's left us.'

I'll spare you the huge screaming row that went on after that. Basically, I said she was lying and that Dad would never leave us, and she said no, she was sorry but it was true, and I said, well then when is he coming back? And she said she didn't know, but probably not in the immediate future, and I said but *wny, why?* And she shook her head and said she couldn't tell me, it was adult stuff, and then I just lost it, and I yelled that it had to be her fault then, that he'd never have left *me*, and she started yelling back—

Never mind. It was *not* a good night.

We went to bed finally, and it was so stupid, but lying awake all I could think about was that Mum hadn't even asked if I had had tea or not. I *had* – Marty's mum had bought us Kentucky Fried Chicken on the way home from the theatre – but she hadn't even asked. It made me feel so alone. Dad would have asked. Dad was the one who held us all together, asking stuff like that. What was going to happen now? How could he have *left?*

I wiped my nose on the sheet. I didn't believe it anyway. They had fights all the time. Dad would be back tomorrow.

Chapter Four

I woke up the next morning and lay there with my eyes closed, listening as hard as I could.

It was still just quiet.

Dad's never quiet. If he's awake, there's music on, even when he's writing. He's got hundreds of CDs he's always playing – classical and jazz and everything. He says he can't think without music. (That's something else they're always scrapping about, because Mum gets tired of the noise. She says of *course* he can think when it's quiet, that quiet is the best place of all to think, and that he's just being perverse. And that if he really can't think without music, then he's a total hazard and they should put it on his driver's licence.)

So the silence downstairs wasn't a good sign.

Except . . . except, except . . . if he and Mum had had such a bad fight, maybe he didn't want to start blaring his CDs right away. Maybe he had just slipped in silently, and was sitting downstairs right now, waiting for us to wake up. I was out of bed and racing downstairs about two seconds after I thought that, practically breaking my neck on the slippery wooden stairs.

Dad wasn't there.

Well, he'd be back soon, obviously. If he stayed at a hotel, they make you leave the next morning, don't they? And it was already after eight.

So I sat down to wait in my favourite chair, the one that's like a big blue pillow. But I hated how quiet it was. A few minutes later I jumped up again and put on one of the CDs, a symphony by someone called Mahler. It's one of his favourites, and in actual fact I don't like it very much, but I felt like hearing it for some reason.

Fifteen minutes later, Mum shuffled downstairs in her bright green dressing-gown, with her short hair sticking up in spikes and her eyes still looking red.

'Jules, what are you doing?' She went to the stereo and turned it down. 'It woke me up, this thing going.'

I shrugged, thinking that *I* woke up because Dad wasn't here, but if *she* could sleep anyway, then she deserved to have horrid old Mahler blasting away at her first thing in the morning.

Mum sat on the sofa and reached for the tissue box again. She blew her nose, and said, 'Jules, you mustn't—'

But just then I heard the rustle and snap of the letterbox, and I scrambled from my chair and dashed down the hall. Because if Dad *wasn't* coming back today, he'd definitely have written to tell me what was going on.

I pounced on the fan of post lying beside the door.

Something from the bank, something from the BBC for Dad—

Nothing. I frowned and looked again, more slowly.

'Jules, I don't think you're going to hear from him just yet,' said Mum from behind me.

I spun round on her. 'Then when? *When?*'

Her hands were jammed in the pockets of her dressing-gown. 'I don't know.'

'He wouldn't just go away and not tell me!'

She took a deep breath. 'I'm sorry. I know how you must . . . look, I just think it might be a while before you hear from him. Trust me, OK?'

Yes, OK. What a good idea. All you've done is drive my dad away and refuse to tell me why, but apart from that, you're *sooo* trustworthy.

And because I didn't even *know* half the words I felt like shouting at her, I threw the post on the floor and went back to bed.

I lay there for a long time, wrapped up in my fluffy white duvet. What was happening? Were they still fighting about me? But why would that make Dad *leave?* My head started to hurt. Finally I got up and sat at my desk, and made a list like Dad says I should do when there's a problem. And this is what I came up with:

1. Dad's already sorry about whatever he and Mum fought about, but he isn't home yet because he's busy shopping on Regent Street. He's buying loads of presents for me and Mum to make up for being gone last night.

I loved thinking about this. I spent ages deciding exactly what he'd buy, and then imagining him flinging the door open, loaded down with mobile phones and CDs and little boxes of jewellery for us both.

But deep down, I didn't really think it was going to happen.

2. Mum's thrown Dad out. She's changed our phone number and the locks. Right this very minute, Dad might be trying to ring, but only getting an 'I'm sorry, this number is not in service' message!!

When I thought of this, I almost started crying when I imagined the look on Dad's face as he tried to ring me. I shoved the list aside and opened my bedroom door a crack. No sound from Mum downstairs. So I sneaked into Dad's study and rang the operator, and asked her if she could tell me what phone number I was ringing from, and she did. And it was ours.

Plus, now that I thought about it, my key had fit in the lock last night when I came home. So that wasn't it.

And then I thought of his mobile, and grabbed the phone again, jabbing in the numbers. I held my breath as it started ringing. Pick up, Dad, pick up! But a recorded voice came on: 'The user is currently unavailable . . .' Oh, how could he not have it switched on? Then I waited and waited for his voicemail message to come on, but it never did. Finally I hung up.

What now? I sat down in Dad's big leather office chair to keep thinking, but for a long time I felt strange and cold and could hardly think at all. I fiddled about with Dad's stapler, pushing the top bit up and down. I kept picturing Dad trying to ring and not being able to. Which was stupid since I knew it wasn't even true.

Suddenly the phone rang.

I almost fell out of my seat grabbing for the receiver. But before I could say hello, I heard Mum's voice saying hello instead, from the downstairs line.

'Holly, hi, how are you?' A Scottish voice. Mum's friend, Jenny.

'Oh, Jenny . . .' Sniffle, sniffle, right on cue. She blew her nose again. I pictured myself nicking her tissue box and grinding hot pepper in it.

'Have you heard from him yet?' Jenny said.

'No, nothing . . . and I just don't know what to tell *Jules*.'

'You can't tell her anything,' said Jenny firmly. 'This is between you and Ben, not Jules.' My jaw fell open. You complete cow!

'But it affects *her* most of all!' said Mum. Yes, *thank you*!

'Of course it does, but Holly, she's only thirteen. How can you tell her such a thing about her own mum? Who knows what it might do to your relationship with her?'

My fingers tightened on the phone. Mum did something terrible. I knew it.

Mum sighed and didn't say anything. Finally Jenny

cleared her throat. 'Is he . . . coming back, do you think?'

'I almost don't care.'

'But—'

'Oh, Jen, come on. All we do is fight.' Mum sounded tired. 'We haven't been getting on for – for I don't even know how long. *Years*. I—'

I banged the phone down, not caring if she heard. God, I wanted to run downstairs and throw something at her! What did she mean, she didn't *care* if Dad came back? What about *me*?

Then all at once it came to me, the reason why I hadn't heard from him. I sat totally still for a second, my mouth open in a little 'o', and then I dashed back to my room to write it down:

3. OK. Mum and Dad have had the fight to end all fights. He's stormed out and he isn't coming back and they're going to get a divorce. BUT, the reason he hasn't rung or written to me yet is that he's too busy finding a new place in London for the two of us to live!!!

That had to be it! He'd come and get me as soon as he found a place – knock on the door, tell me to pack my things and then whisk me away. I was so relieved to have figured it out that I just *flung* myself on my bed, really hard, bouncing up and down and making the bedsprings squeak. I wondered if I should start packing yet. And what would our new place in London be like? Big Ben! The Millennium Wheel, *West End plays!*

Divorce.

I stopped bouncing. Well, I'd see Mum on weekends. Maybe. If she wasn't in Belgium or Japan or somewhere on business. Not that I was that bothered about it, to be honest. I mean, I love Mum, I suppose, even if I hate her at the moment, but Dad's the one who I talk to about everything and who knows all my friends and my favourite foods and all that. He's *Dad*.

And it was all Mum's fault anyway. She didn't even want Dad to come back.

We ate tea in front of the television. If you can call it tea. A soggy cheese omelette and half-burnt chips. Mum kept wiping her eyes and trying to make natural little comments about the quiz show we were watching. Like I was really going to make small talk with her. I kept to my corner of the settee and grunted at her occasionally, and wished Anne Robinson would walk in and tell her off.

The phone rang. Dad! I shot up off the settee and pounded into the kitchen, snatching the phone from the wall: 'Hello?'

'Hello, is that Juliet Cheney?' It was a woman's voice.

'. . . yes, it is.' And it felt just like when we were playing netball once in PE, and I got hit in the stomach.

'Juliet, this is Diane Kosovich. From the Flying Frog Theatre. You gave a very nice audition yesterday, and I wondered if you'd like to come back and read for us again?'

'Um . . . yes, OK.' I had practically forgotten about

the play. It was like something happening on Planet Zog.

'Oh, good. Call-backs are tomorrow at one o'clock. We'll look forward to seeing you then, all right?'

When I went back into the lounge, Mum was staring at me, sitting right up.

'Who was that?'

'No-one.'

'Jules, who *was* it?'

'*No*-one. Just the woman from the theatre.' If you must know.

'Oh.' She sank back down against the cushions. 'What did she say?'

None of your business. 'Thanks but no thanks. Better luck next time.'

'Oh, well . . .' She sniffled again, and shoved at her horrible runny omelette with her fork. 'Never mind. You'll get the next one.'

I just shrugged, and picked up my plate and took it into the kitchen. I'd get *this* one, but I didn't even want Mum to know about it, it was nothing to do with her. It would be a present for Dad, for when he came to get me.

Chapter Five

About thirty kids sat on the stage. Most of them were sprawled together in groups of four or five, chatting away. They all seemed to know each other. I sat by myself trying not to bite my nails, which is a bad habit I have. I wanted to be Lyra so much. It was so important! I imagined myself telling Dad, and how excited he'd be. Maybe he'd even make things up with Mum, and—

Suddenly the lobby door opened and a short, chubby boy trotted down the aisle, huffing and puffing. 'Sorry I'm late,' he gasped to Diane. 'Mum didn't get home in time to drive me.'

Oh, *no!* My eyes bugged right out on stalks, like in the cartoons. Why did *he* have to be here, why why why? I looked away the second he saw me, but it didn't help. Of course.

'Oi, Brickface!' Everyone stopped talking and stared at him. I cringed. Adrian, oblivious, galloped up the stairs and plopped down beside me. 'You made it! Way to go!'

'Yeah, you too,' I muttered. Now everyone was staring at *both* of us.

Finally, Diane put down her clipboard. 'Right, thanks for coming down, everyone.' She ran a hand through her curly hair and gave us a freckly grin. 'Let's get started, shall we?'

She passed out scripts, and sorted us into groups of six. She put me together with Adrian (naturally) and also this older girl called Lesley, with sleek blonde hair and *loads* of poise, like she was studying to be a duchess in her spare time. Diane made her do one of Lyra's speeches first, with a dark-haired boy taking the part of Pantalaimon, Lyra's daemon.

Lesley flipped back her hair as she plunged into the scene. 'Yeah, and what about Roger? We've got to save him!' (Roger is a friend of Lyra's who's been kidnapped by the Gobblers. Most of the book is about Lyra trying to save him.)

They read for a bit, snapping lines back and forth without missing a beat, and I just sat there trying not to gape at Lesley like a complete fool. Because she was *fantastic*. She had totally become Lyra, the fierce, scroungy tomboy – every last bit of her, even down to the tips of her polished pink nails.

I did not have a chance in the world.

'Good,' said Diane. 'OK, Juliet, you read this time, and Adrian, *you* take Pantalaimon's part.' I looked down at the script. My hands were shaking. Adrian elbowed me, and gave me this big smirk all across his round face. 'Ready, *Brick?*'

I was so furious that I forgot to be nervous. And

then once I got into it, I was just Lyra, and – this is even stranger – Adrian was just *Pan*, my daemon, my best friend in the world.

Acting does weird things to you, I can see that already.

On Monday during maths, another note came from Janet Griegson, folded into a fat little triangle with my name on the front.

Where were you yesterday? I rang twice and your mum said you had gone to the library! You NEVER go to the library!

Oh no! I had forgotten all about Marty. We *always* do something on the weekends – go to the shops, or a film, or to each other's houses. Now that I thought about it, it was kind of odd that she hadn't rung on Saturday. But then, she does get into a sulk sometimes, and she had definitely been a bit squiffy with me by the time her mum picked us up on Friday night. This had bothered me at the time, but now it seemed like last Friday was centuries ago.

Marty was sneaking peeks at me, flapping questions with her dark eyebrows. I nibbled on the cap of my pen, wondering what to say. If I told her the truth, she'd feel even worse than she had on Friday, but I couldn't just spin her some bogus tale like I had Mum. She knew me too well.

Finally I wrote, *I just went to the Flying Frog to see if maybe they'd like me to be a stagehand or something.*

40

And passed it back across. That was all I could think of. It wasn't a *complete* lie.

Marty opened the note. She looked at it for a long time, and then over at me. I could feel my face heating up. Just then I was saved by Chatty saying, 'Juliet, would you like to show us how to do this equation?'

Well, sort of saved. I still had to go up in front of everyone and squeak out numbers with the blue dry-marker while Chatty stood to one side, shaking her head and sighing. As if it makes sense to put letters in with numbers in the first place! Finally she said, 'You'll have to do better than that, Juliet. This is on the SATS, you know. Can someone else show Juliet how to do this equation? Adrian?'

Adrian sprang up and raced over to the whiteboard, and as I was turning to go back to my seat, he whispered, 'You were great yesterday, Brickface!' in this really LOUD whisper that probably half the class heard. Marty certainly did, because a few seconds after I sat down again, another note came flying across via Janet:

A great STAGEHAND?!? You are such a liar! You got called back, didn't you?

I didn't answer. I didn't know what to say.

On Mondays we have a double lesson of maths (joy) and then a break right after. So as soon as Chatty set us free, Marty and I went to where we usually hang out, over by the wall where there's some trees. Marty hopped up to sit on the wall and opened a packet of cheese and onion crisps.

'You didn't have to *lie* about it. I think it's great that you got called back.' She looked across the courtyard, where some boys were kicking a football around. 'So . . . are you going to be Lyra? Or what?'

'Don't know yet.' I leaned against the wall next to her. The sun was out for a change, but it was freezing cold. I kept expecting the boys' football to shatter like a giant ice cube.

Marty offered me a crisp. 'How did you do? Were lots of people called back?'

'Well . . . I did OK, I guess. Except I had to read with *Adrian* loads. And . . . guess what?'

'What?'

'There were only two of us called back for Lyra.'

My stomach gave a happy little flutter when I thought about it. It was true. Diane had Lesley and me reading practically all afternoon, and then at the end she took us aside and told us that we were both brilliant and we'd both definitely have parts, and that it was just a matter of which one of us was going to play Lyra. And she'd be in touch soon.

It didn't seem a good idea to mention that bit, actually.

But Marty's face had turned sort of stiff and blank anyway. 'Oh.' She looked down at her crisp packet. 'Well, I think it's great,' she said again. 'Even if you do end up doing it with *Adrian*.'

Then later, at lunch, she hardly said a word to me, she just talked to Janet about Pony Club. And Marty doesn't even have a pony.

*

Dad still wasn't back by then. He had been gone for three days. *Three whole days.* I kept trying his mobile number over and over with no luck at all. After the first day I just got a short, snotty message saying 'the number you have called is not recognized,' whatever *that* means. And yesterday, after I got back from the audition, I even snuck into their bedroom to see if he had sent me an email on Mum's computer.

Nothing.

I don't know why I didn't tell Marty about it. Normally we tell each other everything. Even really personal, *embarrassing* things, like how she does these special exercises so she won't end up flat-chested like her mum, and how I'm scared to get up at night and go to the loo if there's not a light on.

But this time I didn't say a word. No matter what Mum had done, I just wanted it to be another one of their rows that I didn't *have* to make a big deal of talking to Marty about. Because they were always rowing, so what else was new?

Besides, even if things were just as terrible as they seemed, Dad would be getting in touch with me any second now – I mean, there must be some really good reason why he hadn't yet, but he had to *soon*, right? And there'd be loads of time to tell Marty everything then.

Except it didn't happen like that.

When I got home that day, I paused for a minute before I put my key in the lock. I closed my eyes and *willed* Dad to be back, chanting to myself, *I have said it, now let it be done!* But the spell never worked even when Marty and I believed in magic, so I don't know why I thought it might do some good just then.

It turned out to be a total jinx. Almost the first thing I saw when I went into the lounge was that Dad's CD racks were empty.

I just stood there staring. At first I thought we had been robbed, I really did. Dad's CDs practically blanket an entire wall, and now there were only three or four left on every rack, like jagged teeth with lots of empty spaces in between. I went over and looked. The ones left were all Mum's. And a couple of mine. And one or two that I knew Dad didn't like very much.

I dropped my book bag and bolted up the stairs. By then I knew we hadn't been robbed, of course, so first I ran to my room, hoping for a note in Dad's spiky handwriting, or maybe even *Dad himself*, packing my things – but everything was exactly as I had left it that morning. I looked under the pillow, pushed papers and books aside on my desk – nothing. And then I saw that everything wasn't just as I had left it, after all. My hairbrush had been moved.

See, I have this antique silver hairbrush and comb set that Gran gave me, and I always leave them just so on my bureau. But now they were lying any which way, like they had been thrown down. My heart thudded as I stared at them. It was like in a horror film, where ordinary things suddenly loom out at you and become ominous.

I dashed down the corridor to Mum and Dad's room. Dad's wardrobe stood open, empty except for an old sports jacket. I shoved it aside as if the rest of his clothes might be hiding behind it, only of course they weren't. Then I leapt for his bureau, yanking the drawers out one after the other. All empty.

Mum's things were still there, of course. Her jewellery, her crystal clock. The portable CD-player was gone. So was Dad's cologne, and all of his shoes.

Dad was gone. His stuff was gone. He was *gone*.

This sounds daft, but suddenly I *hated* Mum's stuff, sitting there all smug and silent. I grabbed her bottle of Dune perfume from her dressing-table. I don't even know what I was going to do with it. Throw it out the window, maybe, and splatter expensive French perfume all over the street.

But then I saw something really, really strange, and I just stood there holding the perfume, not moving.

We went to Euro Disney last year, you see, and Dad and I went on one of those massive roller coasters that takes you up into the sky and then just *drops* you straight down again. Dad had gone in the seat in front of me on purpose, just so he could turn around and get a snap of me screaming and laughing, with my hair blowing all across my face. It was his absolute favourite photo of me.

And it was still sitting on his bedside table in its silver frame.

I moved slowly towards it, touched its cool smoothness. Dad had forgotten it. How could he have forgotten it?

Well . . . OK. Once I thought about it, it was

obvious. He had been flying around in this searing, massive hurry to get everything packed up before Mum got home, so he wouldn't have to see her. He couldn't even wait to see *me*, he was in such a hurry, so it wasn't surprising that he had forgotten to pack every little thing. I could hardly blame him. I didn't want to see Mum, either. Whatever horrible thing it was she had done, she had *pulverized* our family.

When the Pulverizer got home an hour later, I was waiting for her on the settee. She rushed into the lounge, high heels clicking against the floorboards. 'Oh, Jules, I'm sorry, I meant to be here waiting for you when you got home, but I had a meeting that went on forever—' and then she saw the empty spaces where the CDs used to be.

'Oh no . . .' She just sort of deflated, and sank on to the settee. 'Oh . . . I didn't know he was going to . . .' She dropped her head in her hands, and then looked at the CD racks again with her fingers pressed against her mouth.

'His clothes are gone, too.' I made every word a bullet, zinging them straight at her. 'And his CD-player, and loads of his books. And he left his keys on the dining-room table.'

I didn't mention the photo, which I had already hidden in my room under a pile of summer T-shirts. I knew Dad would be gutted once he realized he didn't have it. I imagined him in some dark, lonely flat somewhere, searching frantically through cardboard boxes. I had to get it to him somehow! Plus . . . plus, could it be *possible* that he didn't know I wanted to be with him? What if Mum had poisoned his mind, telling him I hated him or something? I wouldn't put it past her, I really wouldn't.

I had to find him.

Mum didn't say anything for a long time. She just sat there in her dark grey coat, biting her lip, with her make-up looking brighter and stranger against her face every second. Finally she sniffed, and took a tissue from her briefcase. 'Well, I . . . this says it all, really, doesn't it?'

I watched her through slitty eyes as she blew her nose. Finally she straightened up and took off her coat. Her arms were stiff and slow. 'And this isn't going to work, either,' she murmured. 'A lot of times I don't get home until eight or nine, and you shouldn't be on your own so much . . . we'll have to get someone to come in, I suppose.'

I jumped up from the settee like it was on fire. 'You can hardly wait to start making plans, can you! You don't even *want* him back!'

She winced, and gripped her forehead. 'Jules, please don't scream at me. I'm sorry, I know how you must feel, I *do*, but—'

'What did you do to make him leave? What? Did you have an affair?'

'I *cannot* discuss this with you,' she snapped. 'I'm sorry. I mean it.' She groaned, rubbing her temples. I watched, glaring. Good! I hope she has such a thrashing headache that her head splits open!

Finally she sighed and looked up. 'Jules, can we –

look, there's that curry place you like, why don't we go there for dinner? Would you like to?'

'I don't want to go *anywhere* with you,' I informed her, and I went up to my room and slammed the door as hard as I could. Then I opened it and slammed it again. I hoped the ceiling would crash in! But it didn't. So instead I threw myself on my bed and lay there for ages, imagining horrible punishments for her. Chinese water torture. Boiling in oil.

I bet she *did* have an affair.

Chapter Six

Once I was positive that Mum was asleep that night, I snuck back downstairs and slipped into the kitchen, shutting the door.

Uncle Derek answered on the fifth ring. First there was a crash, like he had knocked the phone over, and then he mumbled, 'H'lo?'

'Uncle Derek, it's me, Jules.' I sat down on the stool under the phone. My hands felt cold. 'Um, is it OK that I rang? So late, I mean? I thought you always stayed up late—'

'That's when I'm in a *play*,' he moaned. 'I'm still taping the series. I have to be on the set at half-six.'

Twelve forty-five, accused the kitchen clock. 'I'm really sorry—'

'What are *you* doing up, anyway?' His voice sharpened into alertness. 'What's wrong?'

'I just—' I took a deep breath. 'Uncle Derek, do you know where Dad is? I have to talk to him, it's really important.'

'What do you mean, do I know where *Ben* is? Isn't he there?'

'No. Not since Friday.' I stared at the clock without blinking, trying not to cry. And shivering a bit, even though I was wearing my thick yellow dressing-gown.

'Tell me everything,' said Uncle Derek after a pause.

So I did. I even told him about Mum's phone call that I overheard, and Dad forgetting my photo.

'Why hasn't he *rung* me?' And I *was* crying by then, I couldn't help it. 'OK, he's mad at Mum, but why hasn't he rung *me*?'

'Darling, I don't know – I—' Uncle Derek cleared his throat. 'I don't know. Probably he just needs some time alone, that's all. He'll get in touch with you soon.'

'But *when*? It's been days! I have to see him, I have to talk to him!'

Uncle Derek sighed. 'Listen, for now – just go back to bed, all right? Try to get some sleep. I'm sure this will all sort itself out. Really. You'll see.'

He didn't sound sure in the least.

Marty grabbed me as I walked into school that morning, her face all shining and flushed. 'Jules, you'll never guess – David Tallis just came up and asked me about the maths assignment!'

I squinted blearily at her, still half-asleep. I hadn't exactly had a cosy night's kip after talking to Uncle Derek. I lay awake for ages thinking, time alone, that's all. Dad just wants some time alone.

But time alone from *me*?

Marty shook my arm. '*Jules!*'

'What?'

'Why would David ask *me* about it? He's *miles* better at maths than me! What do you think? Does he like me?'

Have I mentioned David Tallis? He's this completely weedy geek who's shot up about five inches since Year Eight and probably weighs less than I do. Marty wouldn't have looked at him twice last term. *This* term she goes mad over practically any boy who speaks to her. I find it really tiresome, to be honest, but I wanted to be friends with her again, so we had this long talk about it and decided that he probably *did* like her, and that maybe she should do something to encourage him a bit, like smile at him whenever she could, or try to stand next to him in the lunch queue.

So I thought everything was fine between us again. But then at lunchtime, she looked completely gob-smacked when I said I had to make a phone call. We were walking down the corridor towards the canteen, and she stopped dead in her tracks to stare at me, with kids pushing and streaming all around us.

'But I need you! I can't do it alone! We have to stand there talking casually together, like we just *happen* to be queuing behind him!'

She looked really, really hurt. I felt guilty and annoyed, both at the same time. (I mean, honestly – David *Tallis!*)

'Can we maybe do it tomorrow instead? This phone call's really important.'

Of course she asked why it was so important, and of course I didn't want to tell her. So I said that Dad had urgently asked me to ring about some plans he had for that afternoon, which I don't suppose I'd have believed either, if I had been her. Her face tightened.

'Something to do with being a *stagehand*, is it? You're really turning into a liar, Jules.' She turned and walked away. I really did feel guilty then, and I almost ran after her. But I *had* to find Dad. I dashed to the payphone in front of the office.

While I was lying awake last night, it occurred to me that Dad would have to let the BBC know where he was. They were his bosses, after all. So before I left the house this morning, I sneaked into Dad's study and looked through a bunch of his old business letters until I found one from Pauline Connick, who's in charge of the TV show Dad writes for. (It's called *Never Again*, about this woman who's been married five times.)

I had brought the letter with me, folded up in my blazer pocket. It had loads of phone numbers on it, including the BBC's main number, and also one that said 'direct line'. I tried the direct line one first. I kept my eyes closed tight while it rang, I was wishing so hard.

There was a click, and a voice said: 'Hello, you have reached the voicemail of Pauline Connick. I'm currently away on holiday until Monday, January 30th, but—'

No! I slammed the phone down. Then, when I calmed down a bit, I realized it had been pretty daft to not even listen to the whole message, so I rang again. And the voice went on to say that if you had any queries prior to her return, you could ring her assistant. Then it gave another number, which was gone before I could memorize it, so I had to go borrow a pen from the office and then ring *again*.

When I *finally, finally* got through to the assistant, it was incredibly awkward trying to explain who I was and why I didn't know where Dad was already. I felt like a complete jerk. I stood facing the wall, so no-one could see my face flaming up.

'No, I'm sorry,' said the woman. 'I don't have a new address or phone number down for him. But even if I did, I wouldn't be able to give you that information, I'm afraid. I *am* sorry.'

She really sounded sorry, too, but this didn't make me feel any better. Why wouldn't she be able to tell me? I'm his *daughter*!

Then I tried all the other numbers on the letter, but they were even less use. A lot of them had never even *heard* of Dad, and I kept getting transferred around from person to person and having to explain everything all over again. And then finally the bell rang, and I had to go back to class.

'I *do not* understand your mother.' Granny Sophie rattled pots and pans in the sink menacingly. Great bubbles of washing-up liquid frothed about. 'Wasn't she going to *tell* me Ben had left home?'

'Well—' I shifted my weight and looked longingly at the kitchen door. She had been holding me prisoner ever since I came home from school and found her there in the house. Waiting. And cooking. She had just bunged roast potatoes and a chicken casserole in the oven.

'Um . . . I sort of have homework to do, Gran—'

She rolled right over me. 'Why on earth should I have to hear about such a thing from Derek? *Derek?*' She whipped around and glared at me with glittery black eyes, wiping her hands on a dishtowel. 'And what about you?' she demanded.

I swallowed, thinking she was about to have a go at *me* for not telling her, but instead she said, 'It's nearly six o'clock and your mother's not home yet! Is this how she plans to take care of you?'

Good grief, she was scowling at me like she actually expected an answer! 'Um . . . well, I *am* thirteen.'

Fortunately, the Pulverizer herself arrived home just then. At the first sound of her key in the lock, Granny Sophie flung down the dishtowel and barrelled out of the kitchen. I trailed after her. I must admit, a totally evil part of me really wanted to see Mum get it.

Mum was in the front hallway, shrugging out of her coat. When she saw Gran, she stopped mid-shrug, brown eyes wide. 'Sophie! What are you doing here?'

Gran told her all right. For quite some time.

What possible right did Mum have not to tell her that her own son had left home? Did anyone even know where he *was*? How did Mum think she had felt, hearing about such a thing second-hand from Derek, as though she were some sort of casual acquaintance?

Mum was standing there in a daze, holding her coat. *'Derek?* But—'

Gran didn't even slow down. What on earth was happening? What was Mum doing about it? And what about the child? Did no-one care about *the child*? She swept a dramatic arm towards me. I started to wish I had stayed in the kitchen.

'If I hadn't been here, Juliet would have been alone for *two hours* this afternoon! This will simply not do, Holly!'

Mum stiffened. She hung her coat up, harder than necessary. 'In the first place, my marriage is none of your business. Yes, we're having problems at the moment, but—'

'Problems!'

'But everything is perfectly under control, thank you very much, and although I appreciate your concern over my daughter, please rest assured that *that* is *also* perfectly under control. Jules is more than capable of being on her own on occasion, but as it happens, I've already rung an agency, and we're going to be getting someone to come in in the afternoons, so that—'

'Don't be silly.' Suddenly Gran turned all brisk and no-nonsense, like she was telling Mum the best loo roll to buy. 'You don't need hired help at a time like this, you need family. *I'll* come in the afternoons.'

Mum seemed to notice me for the first time then,

and she gave me this really filthy look, like it was all my fault Gran was there. Which it was, I guess, since I'm the one who told Uncle Derek. I looked coolly back at her. Yeah? So?

She turned back to Gran and took a deep breath. 'Sophie, there's no need—'

'Of course there's a need. I'm happy to help out.' Gran folded her arms across the front of her slithery silk blouse.

'No, Sophie. I mean, thank you, but—'

'The matter is closed. I'll arrive around four and cook dinner for you both every night.'

The phone rang. They both looked at me.

All right, I can take a hint! They were still arguing as I went back into the kitchen, where I dropped onto the high stool and scooped up the receiver. 'Hello?'

'Hello, is that Juliet? This is Diane from the Flying Frog.'

'Oh, hello!' I sprang to my feet again, holding my breath. Oh, *please, please.*

And then she said it! 'I'd like to offer you the part of Lyra.'

'*Really?*' My voice came out in this absolute gasp, and she laughed.

'Yes, really. Is that a yes?'

'Yes, *please!*'

'Wonderful! I think you'll be perfect. Rehearsals start this Saturday at eleven o'clock – I'll look forward to seeing you then.'

I hung up in a daze, my fingers slowly leaving the white plastic. I was Lyra. Oh, *where* was Dad? I wanted to tell him, I had to tell him, he'd be so incredibly happy!

I drifted back out of the kitchen, wrapped up in a lovely private dream: I've just told Dad about getting the part, and he gives this big shout of delight, and scoops me into a bone-crunching hug. He's so over the moon that it jolts him out of needing time alone, and he tells me to pack my things . . .

Mum and Gran had moved into the lounge. Mum was saying, with a tinge of desperation, 'But Sophie, what about your business? You can't just leave it every afternoon!'

'Of course I can; I'm the owner. Gemma is perfectly competent.'

Which isn't what she usually says.

'But your clients—'

'This is *settled*, Holly. Now if you'll excuse me, I believe dinner is ready.' And she turned and marched back into the kitchen.

Mum dropped onto the sofa and groaned. I watched her coldly, feeling a weird sort of satisfaction. She deserved to be told off by Granny Sophie. She deserved much worse than *that*; she deserved *horrible* things to happen to her. Her Prada suits ripped to shreds. To be locked up in jail for ever.

Finally Mum sighed, and peered over at me. 'Who rang?'

I shrugged. 'Just Marty, asking about our maths homework.'

Lyra was for Dad. Not *her*.

Chapter Seven

Marty definitely wasn't talking to me now. Instead she spent all her time with Janet. *Janet*, with her nervous giggle and scraggly fringe! At lunch the next day, the two of them sat all huddled up together, whispering and giggling. I always sit with Marty, but she wasn't even looking at me. So I sat next to her anyway, and then felt like a groupie or something, with both of them ignoring me.

I ripped my carton of orange juice open, wishing I could pour it over Janet's head. It'd add some colour to her hair, anyway.

And then Adrian walked up, holding his tray, and said, 'Hey, Brickface, congratulations!' Marty and Janet stopped whispering and stared at us.

I gave him this *look*, but he's so *incredibly* thick that he didn't get it, and just stood there saying, 'What? Aren't you happy about it, then? I knew you'd get it, you were miles better than Lesley. And guess what, I'm playing Pantalaimon!'

Perfect.

'Great, congratulations,' I mumbled, staring down

at my sausage and chips and not daring to look at Marty. *Finally* he went away, and Marty tossed her dark curls.

'So you're going to be Lyra.'

'Yeah . . . I just heard last night. But Marty, listen—'

'Well, I don't know why you're sitting with us,' she interrupted in this snooty voice. 'We're not *stars* like you and Adrian. You should sit together and plan your *photo-shoot.*'

I wanted to yell at her to stop being such a jealous cow, that it wasn't *my* fault I got the part and she didn't! But I could feel my face going hot and blotchy, so without even looking at her, I just got up and left the canteen, oh-so-slowly-and-casually. Then I ran to the loo and hid out there for ages, crying into a wad of rough, horrid loo roll.

I *hated* Marty! If she didn't want to be friends any more, that was fine with me. Who'd want to be friends with such a jealous cow anyway? She and limp, mousy Janet were made for each other. Janet didn't have anything to be jealous *of.*

When the bell went I was frantically washing my face in the sink, trying to erase my red nose and puffy eyes. It didn't work. Then I was almost late for English. Then of course Mr Haig called on me practically first thing to share my haiku with the class. Everyone turned to look at me.

'I, um – I don't actually have it, sir.'

His bushy rust-coloured eyebrows shot up. 'You didn't do your homework?'

We were supposed to write a haiku that evoked a

feeling the night before, and I thought it was pretty lucky for Mr Haig that I hadn't done it, actually, since my feelings would probably sizzle a hole in the paper and burn his desk to the ground.

'No, sir. I'm sorry, I'll do it tonight.' My face was blazing away like a forest fire, and I knew everyone could tell I'd been crying.

He gave me a long look, and I thought he was really going to tell me off, but all he said was, 'See that you do, Juliet.' I could hear Marty and Janet giggling away like mad behind me.

I bent over my exercise book to hide my face. Forget Marty! Who cared about her, anyway? Dad was the important thing. I had to find him. I *had* to.

On Saturday I told Mum I was going over to Marty's for the day, and then took a bus to the Flying Frog. Simple.

Rehearsals were magic, right from the start. That first day we all sat around the stage, seventeen of us, and Diane passed out our scripts. Thick and weighty and important-looking, with a light blue cover and *Northern Lights* in big letters. My stomach did flip-flops when she handed me mine. I felt like I was holding a Bible, only a million times more exciting.

The empty theatre was starting to feel cosy and natural, like home. Well, *better* than home at the moment, obviously. I loved everything about it, even the dusty, dirty stage.

Diane clapped her hands. 'Right, let's get started.

Everyone, this is Juliet and Adrian, otherwise known as Lyra and Pantalaimon. Stand up, you two, don't be shy.' And then she gave a little speech about how tough the competition had been for both parts, but she knew everyone would do their best to support us, and we were going to have a *brilliant* show. Everyone applauded. I could feel myself getting flushed, but it was sort of nice anyway, even though it was Adrian I was standing up with.

Then we did lots of exercises to get to know each other, silly things like going around the circle and reciting everyone's name in order. When Adrian came to me, he put his finger on his chin and said, 'Ummm – hang on a minute, let me think,' and I knew, I just *knew*, that he was going to call me 'Brickface' and I was going to have to messily slaughter him, all over the stage, but then he came out with 'Jules' right at the last minute. (Perhaps he's not *hopelessly* thick.)

Finally we read through the play, and it was so thrilling that every nerve in my body tingled. Because even though people bumbled their words and there was loads of laughing and kidding around, the story was there, it was *Northern Lights*! Lyra and Pan searching for Roger, being kidnapped by Mrs Coulter and the Gobblers – we were bringing it to life.

I just wished Dad knew about it.

We took a break after the first act, and Lesley drifted over to me, tall and duchess-like. 'Congratulations. You're going to be a super Lyra.'

I felt awkward then, because I probably should have said something to her first. 'Thanks, you're really good, too,' I said shyly.

That was a total understatement. She was playing Mrs Coulter, and she was so absolutely perfect at it, so sparkling and proud and dangerous, that now I couldn't imagine her playing anything else. She was also my understudy, which meant that if I got kidnapped by Martians or something, she'd get to play Lyra after all. I almost told her that I'd try to have a cold just *one* night, so she could do it. But it didn't seem a very tactful thing to mention.

'This is my third Flying Frog show,' she said. She took a sip of Diet Coke. 'I wish I could live here, I love it. Diane's great . . . do you want to be an actress?'

'More than anything,' I said, which wasn't true, since I wanted *Dad* back more than anything, but it was definitely a close second.

Lesley nodded, brushing a stray bit of blonde hair from her face. 'I thought so, you're too good not to do it professionally. My older sister's already an actress – a real one, with an agent and everything. When I'm sixteen, Mum says I can audition for him as well. Two more years, I can hardly wait.'

She kept talking away in this slightly superior way. Meanwhile I don't know what I was doing, I was probably staring at her with my mouth hanging open. I mean, obviously I knew I wasn't *terrible* or else I wouldn't have got the part, but the way Lesley said that, like it was this written-in-stone fact, just completely stunned me.

But then I realized what else she had said. And it was like the sun streaming out after a month of rain.

I knew how to find Dad.

At Monday lunchtime, I was at the payphone in front of the office again, holding the receiver tight against my ear and hardly even daring to swallow. Four rings. Five. Please oh please oh please—

A smooth woman's voice answered. 'Good afternoon, Davison and White, may I help you?'

My heart drummed so loud I could hardly hear myself. 'Yes, please. I need to speak to Mr Davison.'

'May I ask what it's regarding?'

'It's about my father, Benjamin Cheney.'

There was a pause, and then the woman said, 'Hold for a moment, please.'

I put the letter from Davison and White back in my pocket. I'd found it in Dad's study, and it had their address and phone number on it. Then I stood there for what felt like centuries, staring at a bit of graffiti scratched on to the phone. BAZ WOZ ERE. I picked at a piece of flaking paint, turning BAZ into DAZ. Oh, hurry *up*.

Mr Davison is Dad's agent. He handles all of his contracts, and I couldn't believe I had forgotten about him, because I've met him loads of times. Dad's always having him around for dinner, or going out for drinks with him. They're like mates. If anyone in the whole of England knew where Dad was, he would.

'Ian Davison, may I help you?'

I jerked up straight. 'Mr Davison! It's me, Jules, Jules Cheney.'

'Jules, yes. Hello, love, how are you?' His voice sounded deeper than I remembered. And a bit strange, like maybe he had known it was me, but had been *really* hoping it wouldn't be.

'Mr Davison, I need – I have to talk to my dad, it's really important, and I don't know where he is, and I thought – can you tell me, do you have his number?' I could hardly talk, I was so desperate to get the words out.

'Um . . . oh, dear.'

I heard the click of a lighter, and then a long inhale. I knew what it was even over the phone, because he's *always* smoking. Dad says you could get lung cancer just by standing next to him.

'Jules, how much do you know about what's going on?' he said finally.

'Nothing! Just that he's gone, and no-one knows where he is . . .' I kept my eyes glued onto D-for-DAZ, D-for-DAZ, staring at it until it swam and spilled over.

'Right . . . I see.' Another pause, and then Mr Davison sighed. 'Well, love, I'm really sorry, but I can't tell you where he is or his new mobile number. He specifically – well, I just can't. But I'll tell you what. I've got a meeting with him tomorrow morning, and I'll tell him you rang and that you really want to hear from him. All right? Try to talk a bit of sense into him, if I can.'

Tears started running down my face as he spoke. I swiped at my cheek. Some boys passed by, laughing at something, and I pressed right up against the wall so they wouldn't see.

'OK,' I whispered, which was all I could manage without starting to *really* cry. It wasn't fair! I needed to be the one to talk to Dad. Why wouldn't he tell me where my own father was?

'I *am* sorry,' he said as we hung up. Naturally, of course! Everyone was just so, so sorry, but no-one would *do* anything.

And then I had my idea. I stood there still holding on to the phone, my heart doing cartwheels. It was so simple! *I was going to see Dad tomorrow.*

Golden Square is in Soho, which is in the West End of London. It's this small, grassy square surrounded by lots of shops and office buildings that used to be posh houses. Centuries ago. Everything looks sort of crumbly and ancient in Soho.

I sat huddled on a bench staring across at number seventeen, a thin white building with a red door. Cold, cold, cold. I tucked my hands up under my armpits, stamping my feet as my breath froze into little puffs. Some pigeons stood about, watching me hopefully. They looked cold, too.

I'd never done a bunk from school before. It was easy, as it turns out. That morning, I just left the house as usual with my bookbag, and then walked to the train station instead of school. It's only about fifteen minutes from our house. No-one paid me a blind bit of notice, not even the man behind the counter when I bought my ticket.

Jameston is just twenty-five minutes from London, and trains leave all the time, so that part was easy. But when I got to Waterloo Station at just after half eight, there were crowds heaving and pushing at me from every side, and echoing loudspeakers blasting out train times, and I started to panic. It was huge! I'd been there loads of times with Dad, but now I couldn't remember where *anything* was, not even the loo which I was suddenly dying for.

I worked up my courage and asked someone, which turned out to be a good thing because I'd never have found them on my own. After I used them, I asked someone else where the tube was (right in front of me, cringe), and found out I needed to take the Bakerloo Line north to Piccadilly Circus.

The train was dirty and smelled like the loos, and so crowded I could hardly even *see* over all the arms and shoulders pressing against me. My stomach felt like icicles were pricking at it. I stood clutching my bookbag, which had Dad's favourite photo of me in it. What if I missed my stop? What if I just carried on going forever, and got totally lost? I kept stretching up on my toes to see where we were, then falling against people when the train started again.

And then when I got to Piccadilly Circus station, it was shaped like a circular maze and smelled even worse than the train, and there was a ragged, bundled-up man (I think it was a man) asleep on the floor in front of the photo-booth. I was scared to walk past him, to be honest, but no-one else even seemed to notice he was there. But the scariest thing was that there were *six* different exits, all heading out into streets screaming with traffic, and I had no idea which way Golden Square was, not even after looking at the map on the wall. And it was almost nine o'clock, and I had to get there!

I just stood there, practically paralysed, with my throat tight and my eyes stinging and people streaming past me. Then this voice in my head shouted, 'Get a grip! God, you don't even *deserve* to see Dad if you can't work out such a baby problem!'

So I took a deep breath, and stopped a youngish-looking woman wearing jeans. 'Excuse me, can you tell me where Golden Square is?'

She was dead nice, and suddenly everything was OK. She took out an A-Z, and showed me exactly how to get there. She even took me to the right exit. I got a bit turned around anyway, but finally, after crossing Piccadilly Circus twice, and walking down streets with rubbish blowing all about and passing two more people asleep on the pavement, I found Golden Square.

And I settled down to wait for Dad.

Chapter Eight

I sat on the bench holding the photo, not really looking at it, but knowing exactly what it looked like anyway. My biggest problem *then* had been that it was our last day of holiday. Oh, and my stomach had just been turned inside out. Dad and I had got off the ride reeling, laughing and bumping into each other as we tried to walk through the crowds.

'What time are we supposed to meet Mum?' I did a stagger side-step, looking at Dad's watch. I was putting it on a bit by then, and he laughed.

'You look like you've been through a blender.' He ruffled my hair.

I stopped in my tracks, almost knocking over a chubby little boy with a Mickey Mouse balloon. 'Right, where's my hairbrush?' I shrugged my handbag off my shoulders and ferreted about in it.

Dad's nose was sunburnt and freckled. He grinned. 'To answer your question, we're meeting Holly at half past one. So you know what that means.' His brown eyebrows waggled.

I started to giggle as I brushed my hair. The sun

was so bright I had to squint to look at him. 'No, what?'

'It means . . . we have time for another ride! *That one!* Come on!' And he grabbed my hand and we went pelting through the crowd. I shrieked, laughing, still holding my hairbrush, my bag flapping off my arm. Dad's other hand clutched the camera as we ran, keeping it from knocking against his chest.

I shifted on the park bench. Last summer was a million years away. My bum was cold. Everything was cold. I blew on my hands, watching my breath curl about, and wished I hadn't forgotten my hat.

Finally, just before eleven o'clock, I heard a motorcycle roaring up the street. I knew it was Dad, just from the sound of it.

I jumped up from the bench, scattering the pigeons. And sure enough, there he was, driving past in jeans and a leather jacket. He parked his motorcycle and pulled his helmet off, running a hand through his curly brown hair, and I was *pounding* towards him, I was running so hard.

'Dad! Dad!'

His head jerked up like he had been shot. 'Jules?'

He got off his bike just as I flung myself at him, hugging him around the waist and breathing in his leather-jacket smell, so bubbling-over with happiness that it felt like lemonade fizzing through me. He hugged me back, hard. I could feel his breath sort of coming out in gasps, his heartbeat through his T-shirt. Dad, Dad! I'm so glad I came, I'm so glad—

But then it changed. Suddenly he tensed up, taking

me by the shoulders and almost shoving me away from him. 'What are you *doing* here? You didn't come by yourself, did you?'

I gave a tiny nod. The look on his face scared me. His eyes were sad and angry, both at the same time. *Incredibly* sad, and *furiously* angry, like he didn't know whether to cry or hit something. Either one was so unbelievable that I felt dizzy.

'Dad . . .' And there was so much to say that it all choked up inside me, fighting to get out. 'Dad, what's wrong?' I managed.

His jaw tightened, and he snorted and half-turned away. 'What's *wrong!*'

I felt like I was flopping about in the deep end of the pool, trying to find the bottom with my toes and still keep my head over water. 'But if . . . but just because you and Mum had a fight . . .'

'I'm afraid there's more to it than that.'

'Do you need time to think, is that it? Uncle Derek said—'

He turned and stared at me, his eyes hard. '*What* did Derek say?'

I faltered. 'Just . . . just that you might need some time away for a bit. To think. And then you'd be back.'

Dad didn't answer. He leaned against his motorcycle and looked away again, mouth clenched. I touched his arm hesitantly. 'Dad? Dad, listen – the Flying Frog is doing *Northern Lights* as a play. That's why I was going to be late home that Friday, I was trying out for Lyra.'

His face tightened up even worse than when I had mentioned Uncle Derek. I didn't want to carry on at all then, but I had to. 'And – I got it. I'm going to be Lyra.'

His leather jacket squeaked as he folded his arms across his chest. He still wasn't really looking at me. 'Yes, well. I'm not surprised. Well done you.'

I wanted to cry, but everything was cold and numb. I had thought he would be so proud of me! 'Are . . . are you and Mum getting a divorce?'

'Hasn't she got my letter yet?'

I swallowed. 'Letter?'

He glanced at his watch. 'Jules, look . . . I'm going to take you home now, OK? I'm sorry, but this is all – I just can't talk about it.'

'But are you? Getting a divorce?'

He started to say something, then stopped, his eyes skittering away from me. 'Your mother should be getting a letter from my solicitor soon. It'll explain everything.'

We barely said two words to each other on the train home. It was like I had tumbled through a black hole. And everything was too twisted and terrifying to even *think* about, much less talk about. Mostly I just stared out the window. Dad sat beside me concrete-stiff, tapping his fingers on his knee, hardly looking at me.

At Jameston, he put me in a cab for home, telling the driver our address and handing him a fiver. Then he leaned in the back seat and said, 'Jules, believe me, I'm sorry. Look, I—'

He stopped, biting his lip. Finally he gave my shoulder a squeeze and then shut the cab door and walked away.

Suddenly I remembered the photo. I was still holding it! I fumbled with the door handle and shot out of the cab after him. 'Dad, wait!'

When he turned around I thrust the photo at him. 'You forgot this. I knew you'd want to have it, so I brought it with me—'

Dad looked down at the photo and almost shuddered, like it was a photo of a hideous tarantula, and not just me, Jules, shrieking with laughter with my hair blowing everywhere. He warded it off with a rigid hand. 'No, I – you keep it for now, OK?'

My eyes swam as I stood staring at him, holding the photo. He swallowed, and then his hand reached out like he couldn't stop it, tugging at my collar, turning it up. 'You didn't wear a scarf. You know you get throat infections—' He dropped his hand. Turning away, he walked quickly into the station.

He didn't look back.

It had just gone one o'clock when I got home. The house felt like an empty, echoing cavern. I took off my coat and drifted into the lounge. Everything looked sort of not-quite-there. I felt extremely odd, like a ghost, haunting my own house.

The red light flashing on the answerphone snapped me back to myself. Dad, calling from the station! He was sorry he had acted so strange, and now he was on his way to come and get me. I lunged for the phone so fast that I whacked my leg against the coffee table. But when the message started, it was a woman's voice that filled the room.

'Yes, hello, this is Mrs Cole from Highfield Secondary – just ringing to check on Juliet, as she's not in school today. Perhaps someone could ring me back. Many thanks.'

And before I had any time to take *that* in, the machine clicked and whirred, and then burst into a stream of ragged static, with a faint male voice weaving through it. A bad mobile connection? I frowned, trying to make the words out. I missed whole chunks of it, but what I *did* hear was bad enough.

'Hello, Holly, it's me *crackle, snap* . . . get together tomorrow night? It's really important that I see you *snap, static, snap* . . . I'll pick you up at seven *static, whine* . . . something to eat, and then maybe back to my place. Anyway, *whine, crackle* . . . all, really. 'Bye for now, darling.'

I knew she was having an affair, I *knew* it! I stabbed the rewind button as hard as I could, erasing the voice, *destroying* it. Darling! Back to his place! How *could* she?

I grabbed my bookbag and ran up to my room. I hurled it in the back of my wardrobe and hoped the glass on the stupid photo would break. Then without planning it, I started throwing clothes into my rucksack. I wouldn't stay here, no-one could make me. It was all her fault, *all of it*. I'd be sick if I had to talk to her. Or look at her. Or think about her.

Three pairs of jeans. Five jumpers. Socks, knickers, my copy of *Northern Lights*, my script, my favourite blue T-shirt (which obviously I wouldn't need in January, but I wasn't really thinking). Eeyore, my stuffed bear. He barely fit in at that point, everything was so bulging. I had to really jam him in, and even then part of his head stuck out once I had done up the zips as far as they would go – one golden-brown eye, looking alarmed. Stupid to take him, I know, but Dad gave him to me. I couldn't just leave him.

Then I put on the necklace Dad gave me last Christmas – a little sapphire star on a gold chain. I was only supposed to wear it on special occasions, but forget *that*. I'd die before I left it.

The photo lying buried in my wardrobe flashed into my mind. Dad . . .

I pushed the thought away before I could start crying again, which I was really tired of doing. I put on the rucksack (how can clothes weigh so much?) and went into Mum's bedroom.

She always keeps an emergency twenty pounds in her jewellery box. And sure enough, there it was when I opened the little tray at the bottom, where her earrings are – a flash of silver and purple with Queen Elizabeth's face on it. Mum is big on *emergency* this and that, which is pretty funny given that our entire lives are in this roaring state of emergency now, and all she's doing about it is oozing off to dinner with a *boyfriend*.

I put the twenty pounds in my back pocket, which gave me a bit of a twinge, but not much. I thought of writing a note, but what was there to say? *Have fun on your date, Mum. Say hello to your new flame for me.* I put on my coat and walked out into the grey winter day, closing the front door behind me. *Click*, goodbye. Good riddance.

I didn't have much of a plan. I just walked towards the high street, because that's the way I always go. It seemed a lot further this time, with the rucksack straps gouging into my shoulders. I imagined poor Eeyore looking out, wondering what on earth was going on.

A long queue stood at the bus stop. Women wearing big bundly coats and carrying shopping bags, nattering away to each other. None of them seemed to notice me – or at any rate, none of them pounced on me and said, 'Ere, shouldn't you be in school, love?'

I joined the queue and stood there biting my thumbnail, watching the traffic pass by on Winston Road and wondering where I should go. Gran would be at our house at four, and Mum a few hours after that. Where could I go that they wouldn't just find me and drag me back again?

Then it came to me. And it was perfect, because it was the only place I really wanted to go, anyway. So when a number 32 came, I took it to the Flying Frog.

Adrian and I crouched together at one end of the stage: Lyra and Pan, hiding in a pretend wardrobe. I watched nervously as Mike, the tall boy who plays Lord Asriel, picked up a coffee cup from the table at the centre of the stage. He held it to his lips.

'No!' I gasped.

He put the cup down, frowning in our direction. 'Who's there?'

I burst out of hiding and grabbed the cup from his hands, throwing it downstage. It clattered and bounced. Mike gripped my wrist, jerking me backwards. 'Lyra! What are you doing here?'

'Let go of me!' I struggled wildly against him. (He wasn't actually holding me that hard.)

'Um . . . um, um . . .' Mike dropped my wrist and frowned down at his script. 'Hang on . . .' He turned the page.

'How dare you come in here?' I said.

'Oh, yeah.' He grabbed my wrist again and scowled. 'How dare you come in here, you little clever clogs?'

'I've just saved your life!' I shouted, except that I started spluttering with laughter halfway through. 'The wine was – was—' I doubled over, holding my stomach and gasping for breath between shrieks.

Mike and Adrian started laughing too. 'The wine *was*? Was what? Eh? Spit it out, daughter,' said Mike.

'All right, all right,' called Diane from the front row. She was smiling. 'Start again, from "No!" '

We did the whole scene four more times: me convincing Pan to sneak into the forbidden Retiring Room, then hiding in the wardrobe so we wouldn't get caught. Seeing one of the Masters poison Lord Asriel's wine; dashing out to save him, imploring him to believe me . . .

It was indescribably lovely being Lyra. She didn't

have a single problem that she couldn't solve by herself.

Naturally, the moment we took a break that night, Adrian came up to me and asked, 'Why weren't you in school today?'

'Oh, just this family thing.' I shoved some change into the drinks machine. Coffee with milk. I like coffee sometimes. Only not from drinks machines, as it turned out.

Adrian's mouth opened again. Before he could ask what 'a family thing' meant, I waved at Lesley and walked away, leaving him standing there.

When rehearsal ended at nine o'clock, I wandered off to the ladies' loo backstage, dum dee dum, not a care in the world. I closed myself in one of the stalls, perched up on the toilet so my legs wouldn't show, and then just sat there reading my script, waiting for everyone to leave. Except that I couldn't concentrate on my script much. What was I going to do?

Don't laugh, but I had this vague idea that maybe I could hide out in the theatre, *living* there. Mum didn't know I was in the play, so there wasn't any reason why she'd think of coming here to find me. Maybe I could actually do it. Like these kids in a book I once read, who lived in a museum in New York City. Although it's probably the sort of thing that only ever works in books. And, to be honest, the more I thought about it, the more the idea of being alone in the dark theatre was seriously starting to scare me.

But where else could I go? I bit my nail. I had already spent hours that afternoon wandering around the neighbourhood waiting for the rehearsal to start (shifting my brick-filled rucksack from hand to hand). The Flying Frog was in the middle of loads of businesses and pubs; it wasn't like there was anywhere to hide out overnight where I wouldn't freeze to death.

Suddenly there were footsteps, and the door to the loo opened. I tensed and waited for someone to come in. Instead the lights snapped off. The door banged closed again, and the footsteps faded.

Right, OK . . . don't panic. I'd count to a thousand to give whoever it was time to go away, and then I'd sneak out of the theatre and . . . what? Never mind, just count!

One . . . two . . . three . . .

It was so *dark*. I couldn't even see the cubicle I was sitting in. I closed my eyes and tried not to think about it, but by the time I got to forty-two, I couldn't stand it anymore. I fumbled for the lock and let myself out of the cubicle. And then I couldn't find the *door*. Oh, help, *help* – I held my breath and groped about the loo, waving my hands in front of me and expecting to touch something horrible any second. Finally I bumped into the sinks. I felt my way over to the door and cracked it open.

Relief! Light! Not much, but *some*. The fairy lights were on. They're set in plastic runners along the backstage floor, so you can see where you're going during a performance. They turned everything shadowy and strange. Old bits of props loomed from the darkness: a flat wooden rosebush from when they did *Alice*, a section of stone wall from *The Secret Garden*. I tiptoed past them, stopping and listening with every step. All I could hear was my heart pounding in my ears.

I finally got to the front of the stage and looked out into the empty theatre. Except it wasn't quite empty – there was still a light on, high up above in the sound booth. And then my heart forgot about pounding in my ears, and flew into my throat instead. *Something had moved up there!* Diane, it had to be Diane—

The light went out.

I scrambled down the stairs and raced up the aisle through the theatre, grabbing my rucksack from its hiding place and scooting out of the door. In the lobby, only the light inside the ticket booth was still on. The front door hadn't been locked yet, and I hardly even stopped, I crashed through it so hard.

Suddenly I was out in the cold January night, with the sky all strange and orange from the streetlights. Keep moving, don't hang about. I put on my rucksack as I started up the street.

But after about ten steps, I realized that it was even scarier out *here* than in the theatre. Pubs I had hardly even noticed that afternoon were lit up and noisy, with drunk, laughing people spilling out of them. And – my stomach turned to icy slush – there were three dark figures heading towards me down the street. I fled around the side of the theatre, pressing against the wall until they passed. Teenage boys, shouting and shoving each other.

I let out a shaky breath. I reached up and touched Eeyore's nose, just to feel him there. I was *not* going home, not with Mum going out on dates, and Dad *gone* – not even wanting to see me, or – no! I was *not* going to think about it. I shivered against the cold brick. Oh, *why* hadn't I stayed in the theatre? It was just Diane, you jerk! I peeked around the corner back at the Flying Frog, wondering if I should slip back inside after all.

But I didn't get the chance, because just then Diane came out of the theatre and locked the door.

Chapter Nine

I stood there gaping for probably five minutes – anyway, long after Diane got into a little Ford Fiesta and puttered away. What *now?*

When I was sure Diane had really gone, I went and tried the door anyway. All that happened was that it rattled as I pulled at it. Big surprise. I stood in the doorway and looked around, hugging myself.

A spicy, flowery curry-scent wafted out from a restaurant across the street. And suddenly I was *starving*. My mouth watered as I thought of onion bhajis, chicken tikka, naan bread. I sort of swayed, staring at the restaurant. But I had to make my twenty pounds last . . .

Just then the door to the restaurant opened, and someone started jogging across the road, straight towards me.

I snapped back into the doorway and tried to hide in the shadows, but with all the streetlights there weren't many of them. I closed my eyes, pressing against the cold stone as hard as I could. The running footsteps grew closer, and closer . . . and stopped.

And oh no, oh my God, I could hear someone standing right there next to me, I could hear them breathing . . . I turned my face away and tried not to *whimper* with terror.

'Brickface . . .?' said a voice.

My eyes flew open. Fury, relief! '*Adrian!*'

He drew back a bit. I guess he could tell I was either about to murder him or burst into tears. 'I mean – Jules. What are you doing here still?'

I sniffed, and wiped my nose. 'I'm waiting for my mum to come and get me. She's a bit late.'

'My mum would give you a lift, I bet. We're just waiting for our takeaway across the street.'

'No! No, thank you. I'm fine. Really.' This couldn't be *happening*. Adrian Benton, of all people. Go away, leave me alone!

He didn't, of course. He just stood there, shifting about from foot to foot, chubby and awkward. For once, at least, he wasn't smirking cheesily at me. Finally he said, 'Why were you trying to get into the theatre?'

'I wasn't.'

'Yes, you were, I saw you.'

'I just – I left something inside. No big deal. I'll get it tomorrow.'

He looked doubtfully at my bulging backpack. 'Are you, um – well, look, is something wrong? Because, I mean, you shouldn't be out here alone, and—'

'So what? What's it to you? Just go *away*, why can't you?' I was so frustrated and fed up that I actually stamped my foot at him. 'Go *away!* Leave me *alone!*'

My throat choked up. I turned quickly towards the wall with a hand over my eyes, sniffling against the sting of tears and *hating* Adrian.

'Adie, *there* you are!' said a woman's voice. 'I looked around and you had vanished. What's going on?'

Buzzing whispers as Adrian blurted everything out to Mummy. Though I hardly even cared at that point. Then I felt a hand on my arm, and his mum gently turned me towards her. She wasn't as chubby as he was, but she looked round and comfortable, with soft brown hair.

'There now, love!' she said. 'It can't be *that* bad, can it?' She put her arms around me, and suddenly that was all I could take, and I just crumpled against her shoulder and started to cry. I didn't even care that Adrian was standing there watching.

To make a long (and hideously embarrassing) story short, Mrs Benton asked me if Mum was really coming to get me, and when I said no, she insisted that I go home with her and Adrian. And I was so cold and tired and hungry that I just said OK and got in the car with them.

They lived in a terraced flat a mile or so away, over in Northton. Their street looked dead shabby and depressing as we turned into it – overflowing bins everywhere, great loops of graffiti.

As we walked up dark, cramped stairs to their first-floor flat, I started feeling really sorry for Adrian. He had got quieter and quieter, and now he was sort of hanging back, cringing as his mum dug about in her handbag for the keys. Obviously their flat was some sort of horrible hole. I steeled myself to smile and say it was nice no matter what.

But then we got inside, and it was a genie's lair! Rainbow silk draped from the walls and ceiling in billowing clouds, and big plush pillows with silken tassels piled everywhere. And a lovely smell, like jasmine perfume. I stood there staring, trying to get my head around the fact that *Adrian* lived in this magic place.

'It's *lovely*,' I breathed.

Adrian shrugged, relaxing a bit and smiling at me. 'A bit weird.'

'Now, then,' said Mrs Benton. She took her coat off. Under it she wore jeans and a loose top covered in red and blue embroidery. 'Just sit back and relax, you two. We'll have a bite to eat and then decide what to do, shall we? Adie, would you fetch the table?'

Adrian went into another room and brought out a low black table, and we pulled cushions round and tucked into the curry. (There was loads, which was good since I made a total pig of myself.)

'How was the rehearsal?' asked his mum.

Adrian grinned at me. 'Great.' And then he went into this imitation of Mike forgetting his lines and me reminding him, and it was even funnier hearing him tell the story than it had been living it the first time.

'No, that's not how it went! It was like this.' I scrambled to my feet and became Lyra again, bursting out from the wardrobe. 'No!'

Adrian turned into Mike, raising his eyebrows. 'Um – Lisa? Or, um – Lesley? Oh dear, what's your name again? Where's my script?'

'Lyra!' I shrieked. 'Your daughter! And I just saved your life!'

'*Did* you?' Adrian looked astounded. He stared mournfully down at the floor. 'And here I thought you just spilled some rather good wine . . .'

Adrian's mum was rocking with laughter, clutching a knee to her chest. 'Bravo! I hope the actual play's as good as that.'

We sat down again, Adrian bouncing and beaming. I smiled at him, feeling almost happy.

After we finished dinner, Mrs Benton settled back on her cushion, tucking her feet up under her as she lit a cigarette. She winked at us. 'Don't tell the authorities on me about the second-hand smoke.' She poured herself some wine. 'Right, then. What are we going to do with you, Jules? I'm sure your parents are worried—'

'I'm not going back home,' I said instantly. 'I won't. I'm not.'

'Mmm. Let me think.' Her round face creased a bit as she puffed on her cigarette. 'Will you tell me what's happened?' she asked finally.

I glanced at Adrian, who sat munching on a piece of naan bread. His mum read my mind. 'Go off and do some homework, Ade. We've got girls' talk to do in here.'

I told her all of it. I cried loads, and Mrs Benton

handed me pale green tissues and cried a bit too, and told me to call her Wendy.

When I finally finished, Wendy shook her head and lit another cigarette. 'You poor love, what a rotten mess.' She sighed. 'Listen, you're not going to like this, but I'm going to have to ring your mum, I'm afraid.'

'I'm *not* going home! How *can* I, with Mum seeing someone else – and—'

'Don't start again, love, there's hardly any tissues left!' She leaned over and dabbed at my eyes. 'Just hear me out. You see, I could get into a lot of trouble if I didn't tell someone where you are. They might even call it kidnapping.'

Oh.

'You could ring my Uncle Derek, maybe,' I suggested weakly.

'Could you stay with him, d'you think?'

'Um . . . I don't know.' I picked at the cushion's blue tassel. Uncle Derek wasn't actually home very much; he was always on tour or something. Couldn't I stay with *you?* I wanted to ask. Live here for ever in the genie's lair? But I was too shy to ask.

She stubbed her cigarette out on a saucer and we sat silently for a few minutes. She had turned the electric fire on, and the room felt warm and snug. Finally Wendy put her hand over mine and gave it a squeeze. 'Jules, I'm going to have to ring your mum. I'm sorry.'

So I gave her our number. And then I heard myself blurt out, 'Don't tell her that I saw Dad, OK? Please?'

Wendy smiled and touched my head as she stood

up. She had such nice brown eyes, like warm chocolate. Adrian was *lucky*.

The phone was over in the corner, on some sort of Greek pedestal thing. 'Hello, is that Mrs Cheney?' Wendy winked at me. 'Yes, hello. This is Wendy Benton; my son is a friend of your daughter's. Jules has been here for an hour or so—' She stopped abruptly. I winced. I could hear the agitated buzz of Mum's voice, even from all the way across the room. Wendy didn't seem ruffled at all. She just took another sip of her wine.

'Oh, I know. Yes, of course; I'd be *wild* if it were Adrian! But she's been very upset, I'm afraid, and she's only just now given me your number . . .'

The buzz retreated a bit. Wendy gave Mum directions to her flat. Then, just at the end, Wendy's eyes flew to mine and held them as she said, 'I don't know. Just wandering about all day, I think. Then this evening she went to play rehearsal.' Pause. 'Oh? Well, she and Adrian are in a play together at the Flying Frog.'

I squirmed a bit on my cushion. I had forgotten to ask her not to mention *that*, either.

Mum must have broken speed records to get to Wendy's, because she turned up about twenty minutes later, her face white and strained. She scooped me into a hug which I did *not* return, and then said, 'Come on, let's get you home.'

Instead of replying, I turned and gave Wendy a massive hug goodbye. 'I don't want to go!'

She rubbed my back. 'It'll be OK,' she soothed. I pressed against her. Off to the side, I could see strips of pink and purple silk shimmering in the draught from the door.

Finally Mum took my arm. 'Thank you for all your help,' she said to Wendy. 'Come on, Jules. It's time to go.'

I walked out without looking at her once.

Outside, I waited for the explosion, but Mum didn't say a word as we got in the car. Finally, when we were stopped at a red light a few streets away, she cleared her throat. 'Why didn't you tell me you're in a play?'

I shrugged without looking at her.

'It's *Northern Lights*, isn't it? The one you tried out for.'

'I'm just an extra,' I said coldly. 'Nothing important.'

The light turned green and she pulled away, yellow streetlights playing across her face. I stared out the window at the passing shops.

When we got home, Granny Sophie was there. First she grabbed me up in a fierce smothering hug, and then she started shaking me so hard that my teeth chattered. 'You stupid, stupid girl! What did you think you were doing, worrying us like that? Not going to school, not even a *note* – don't you know what *happens* to stupid little girls who wander about the streets by themselves?'

She was in a right old state, dark eyes snapping at me, her fingernails clenching my shoulders. I swallowed. I couldn't say a word.

Finally, Mum stepped in, and gently pulled me away. 'She's safe now, Sophie. Why don't you go home and get some rest? It's been a long, horrible day.' She looked at me. 'For all of us, probably.'

So the explosion never came. Not even the next morning at breakfast.

I gave Mum short, hard glares as she sipped a cup of coffee, her face still drawn. Go on, shout at me for running away! I could hardly *wait*. I'd tell her *exactly* why I left – that I knew all about her seedy, sordid affair, knew all about her boyfriend and how she had smashed our family to smithereens.

But she never asked.

As we cleared away the breakfast plates, she said, 'I'm going to go in with you this morning and have a quick word with Mrs Gray. I'd rather you weren't punished for skipping school yesterday, and I'm going to tell her that.' She looked at me with a strange, pleading expression in her eyes. Well, if she was hoping for some big grateful response, she'd be waiting a long time.

'I suppose you mean Mrs *Greaves*,' I said.

Mum flushed slightly. She turned to the bin and brushed crusts and crumbs off the plates. 'Mrs Greaves, then.'

She never even mentioned her twenty pounds. I slipped it back in her jewellery box when she wasn't looking.

Chapter Ten

Thankfully, Highfield Secondary is absolutely massive, with about a dozen buildings, and the head's office is in a completely different place from where I needed to go for my first class, which was in the art building. So at least I was spared everyone in my group seeing me walking into school with my mummy.

Not that things were that great anyway. The moment I walked into the building, Vicki Young came up to me and cooed, 'Well congratulations, Jules! I hear you're a big stage star now.'

Georgina said, 'Maybe she'd even give us her *autograph* if we asked her really, really nicely. If we begged and pleaded.'

Vicki put on an awestruck face. 'D'you think she really *would*? A big star like her?'

Later, of course, I thought of loads of cutting, brilliant comebacks. But with both of them standing there sniggering at me, I just flamed up and couldn't say a word. I tried to shove past them, but they blocked my way. They're both miles taller than me.

'Oooh, she's far too famous to talk to *us*,' said Vicki.

'Little Miss Star,' agreed Georgina. '*Very* little. Midget-sized, in fact.'

I had turned to go back in the other direction, towards the loos, but now I whirled at them and said, 'I'm not! I just have a part in a play, that's all. It's no big deal.'

'Well, that's not what *I* hear,' said Vicki, flipping her hair back. '*I* hear that it's such a big deal that you've turned dead superior over it.'

Marty.

'I *haven't.*'

Then, just to make everything that much more wonderful, Adrian came up.

'Hi, Jules!' His jacket and tie were all rumpled, as usual. He smiled expectantly, ignoring Vicki.

She smiled. 'Oh, *sorry* to interrupt! We'll let you talk to your *co-star* in peace, shall we?' They walked off laughing.

Panic hit my stomach. I didn't want to talk to Adrian. He had seen me crying with a *teddy bear* in my rucksack! So before he could say a word, I said, 'Look, I have to go to – um, the library, but say thanks to Wendy, I mean, your mum, will you?'

I started to move away. He didn't get it. He just started walking with me, grinning happily. 'Yeah, OK. Listen, Jules, do you want to come around sometime, like on a Sunday maybe? We could watch videos, or play games on my Atari.'

My face burned. I mean, maybe he had been OK the other night, but he was still round, bumbling *Adrian*. The dregs of Year Nine. I heard myself blurt out,

'Adrian, look, I really don't want to be friends, OK? I'm sorry.'

I rushed off, not wanting to think about how his smile had faded. And how hurt his brown eyes had looked.

Everything just got worse as the day went on. Marty and Janet walked to all their classes together, ignoring me. I didn't have anyone to sit with at lunch. And Vicki and her lot ploughed into me really hard in the halls, on purpose. And then just smirked and said, oooh, *sorry*, Jules.

Maybe I could change schools.

Mum picked me up that afternoon, pulling up beside me and beeping the horn as I started to walk home. At first I just stopped and stared at her. I mean, come *on* – had she actually taken time off work to pick me up at school when I can *walk* home?

She leaned across the passenger seat and opened the door. 'Get in.'

Fine. I got in and slammed the door. I suppose I can't be trusted anymore, can I? I might hitchhike to California if she didn't keep an eye on me. I *wish*.

We drove home without talking, Mum clearing her throat every now and then, like she wanted to say something. Clear away, I couldn't care less. I was too busy getting matey with the car window, memorizing every line and mark on it.

I started to go up to my room once we got home, but Mum stopped me with a hand on my arm. 'I need to talk to you, Jules.'

Right, so here it comes. I jerked away from her and stalked into the lounge, where I threw myself into the big blue chair. *Not* the settee. Let her sit by herself.

Mum sank down on the cushions and lit a cigarette. For a long moment she just sat there, sort of huddled up, staring at her hands. Her short dark hair looked limp and tired. I sat watching her frostily.

Finally she looked at me. Her lips twitched upwards a bit. 'I've had to – well, I've been doing a lot of thinking. Things have to change. *I* have to change.'

Please do. Into a human being would be nice. I heaved a sigh and looked at the ceiling, crossing my arms over my chest. Mum kept on, her voice low and measured.

'When Sophie got here yesterday afternoon and you weren't here, she rang me at work. And – you can't imagine how I felt , Jules. The absolute panic. By the time I got home, she had spoken to your school, and rung the police – and they didn't come over, they don't unless you've been gone longer than just a few hours, but they suggested that we ring your friends and see if they knew where you were. And—'

Her voice dropped. 'And I realized that I don't know any of your friends,' she said huskily. 'I know Marty, but not her surname. I don't know where she lives, or what her number is. I've never met her mother. And I don't have a clue who any of your other friends are. Ben was the one who . . . and I don't even know where he *is*, so I couldn't ring him, or . . .'

Mum's voice trailed off. I tightened myself. *No way* was she going to make me feel sorry for her.

She wiped away a tear, and sniffed. 'It was a horrible, horrible night. I had to face the fact that I haven't been a very good mother to you. That I hardly know the first thing about your life.' She tried to smile. 'That I don't even know whether your headmistress is called Mrs Gray or Mrs Greaves.'

I shrugged, still staring up at the ceiling. This was all just *sooo* touching.

Mum took a long drag on her cigarette and stubbed it out in the brass ashtray. She blew out a slow stream of smoke.

'Anyway, things are going to change. I had a long talk with my boss today, and I'm going to be working a lot fewer hours from now on. I'm turning some of my clients over to colleagues, and a lot of what I have left I'll be able to do from home, on the computer. It's quite common nowadays apparently – it's called telecommuting. Sort of funny, I thought.' Her smile was a hesitant invitation.

Yes, ho ho. 'What about Granny Sophie?' I flung out.

Mum shook her head. 'No, that's what I'm explaining to you – Granny Sophie won't be coming in the afternoons anymore. I'll be here. I'll be driving you to school, and to play practice. All of that.' Her expression became wistful. 'I know you're angry at me right now, Jules, and fair enough, but I'm going to be a proper mum to you from now on, whether you like it or not.'

'Great,' I said. 'Can I go now?'

She gave me a long, level look. 'No, not yet.

There's something else. I got a letter from your father's solicitor at work today. He's . . .' She took a deep breath. 'Jules, your father has filed for divorce.'

Well. It wasn't exactly a surprise. But my stomach jerked anyway, and I couldn't say anything for a minute. I didn't let my expression change. I didn't want sympathy, not from *her*.

'Did he say anything about me?' I asked.

Mum looked down at her hands, which were twitching like they didn't know what to do without a cigarette. 'No,' she said finally.

Upstairs at my desk, I plunged into my mountain of homework. Two days' worth of horrible x's and y's for Chatty. A chart of the annual rainfall in Brazil; a paragraph on Mary, Queen of Scots. Riveting stuff. Finally I got it all finished, and went downstairs to get some juice. I found Mum with her reading glasses on, squinting at a cookbook. A cutting-board covered with chopped onions and peppers sat on the counter, and a pot of water bubbled on the hob.

Apparently being a proper mum actually involves cooking, instead of just slapping sausages into a saucepan and cranking up the oven for oven chips.

I took out the orange juice and shoved the fridge door shut. 'What are you doing?'

'Cooking tea, of course.' She opened a package of chicken breasts and started chopping them into slow, laborious cubes, frowning in concentration.

I watched her struggling away for a bit, and then I said, in this really innocent voice, 'But what about your *date*?'

Ha! That got her, all right. Her head snapped towards me, eyes wide. 'My what?'

'Your *date*. Don't you remember? There was a message on the machine yesterday: a man's voice, all about you going out with him tonight—'

'Oh, *Jules*.' Mum took off her reading glasses. 'Is *that* why you ran away? Sweetie, that was Uncle Derek.'

I snorted. Oh, please.

She turned back to the chicken. 'Well, you can ask him yourself the next time you see him, if you like. We were supposed to be going out to dinner tonight, to talk about this whole mess with Ben, but we had lunch today instead.'

I just stood there holding the half-empty glass, staring at her. Remembering all the static and how hard it had been to understand the message. 'But – he called you darling—'

Mum shook her head impatiently. 'He calls *everyone* darling, silly.'

Which was true, actually, but even so, I suddenly felt dizzy with fury. I banged the glass onto the counter and slammed out of the kitchen. OK, fine, maybe the voice on the machine *hadn't* been whoever she's having an affair with – but I still bet she's having one. She's done *something* terrible. Why else would Dad be divorcing her?

Mum drove me to school again the next morning. It was like being a prisoner, escorted about by the police. I sat with my arms crossed, staring out the window again.

She cleared her throat. 'By the way, I forgot to mention . . . you have a doctor's appointment today at five.'

I frowned at her. 'What for? I'm not ill.'

'Yes, I know.' She shifted gears, not looking at me. 'It's just a check-up. But don't hang about after school, OK?'

After the last bell, I walked ve-ry ve-ry slo-o-o-wly to my locker. Which I hardly ever use, but it's on the other side of the school from the car park. I put all my books in. Then I took them out again. Then I arranged them in my bookbag and took them out again and rearranged them. Finally, I meandered out to the car park, going the long way, so that I walked all the way around the gym and playing fields.

The playing fields take a really, really long time to walk around.

Mum was standing beside the car with steam pouring out of her ears. 'What *took* you so long? Get in!'

We were two minutes early to the doctor's even so, not that it mattered. At five-thirty we were still sitting in the waiting room. I flipped through a magazine. *Ten ways to tell if your lover is cheating on you.* I narrowed my eyebrows *significantly* at Mum, only I don't think she noticed. She sat on the edge of her seat, watching the clock and fidgeting about with the clasp on her handbag.

When they called my name, she sprang up and grabbed my hand. Honestly! I yanked it back. 'Do you *mind?* I'm not a three-year-old!'

Dr Jordan took her glasses off and smiled at me as we walked in. 'Hello, Jules! How are you?'

'*Fine.*' I sat down and ignored Mum, who sort of hovered to one side, lips pressed together.

'Right now, let's get you sorted. This will just take a moment.' Dr Jordan took a syringe out of a little plastic packet. Its pointed tip gleamed.

Every muscle in my body tensed up. 'What's that for?'

She took my arm and swabbed it with a cold, prickly liquid. 'We're just going to take a little blood for a blood test, that's all. Just look away; it won't hurt.'

'But—'

'Just look away.'

I stared at Mum, who tried to smile, except that her eyes looked as wide as mine. Suddenly I winced as the needle jabbed into me. And I'm not a baby, right, but it *hurt*, and my eyes filled with tears.

'There, all done!' said Dr Jordan. She popped a plaster on my arm. 'That wasn't so bad, was it?' I didn't answer. No, it was great, I really enjoyed it. Can I have another go?

'Why do I need a blood test?' I demanded, the second we were out of the surgery. Mum became dead engrossed with rummaging about in her handbag for the parking slip.

'It's nothing. Just routine. They like to have it for their files.'

'Marty hasn't had to have one!'

'Jules, I promise, it's nothing.' Mum snapped her handbag closed and strode ahead to the parking fee machine. She fed it coins without looking at me.

Maybe I had some sort of disease. Something terrible, where bits of you turn black and fall off. Would that make Dad leave? Maybe he knew I was going to *die*, and couldn't bear to be around me anymore. Leprosy. Or polio. Or typhus. I lagged behind as we walked to the car.

My arm hurt.

'So we divide out four from both sides of the equation – like so – and *that* leaves us with x equals three. Does everyone understand?'

Chatty turned and scanned her gaze over us: a forest of blank, bored faces. 'Right. Let's try another one, shall we?' She squeaked more numbers and words on the whiteboard with her blue dry-marker. 'Two trains leave Edinburgh at 12 o'clock. If train Y goes at ninety miles an hour, and train X goes at sixty miles an hour . . .'

The plaster had been off my arm for two days now, but there was still a bruise, sore and mottled, with a swollen pinprick at the centre. Just how I felt. I sneaked a glance at Marty. She looked bored, doodling flowers across her notes.

I wish I could talk to her about all of this! Why was she being such a total jerk? I could be dying from some creepy plague; my parents were getting divorced; Dad was *gone*. Before I could think about it and change my mind, I pulled a piece of paper from my binder and wrote:

> Marty,
> I'm really, really sorry about everything. Please can't we be friends again? There's so much I need to talk to you about. I miss you!
> Jules xx

I passed it to Janet, folded up tight with Marty's name on the front. Janet's eyebrows shot right up into her wispy fringe, like she couldn't *believe* I was passing notes to *her* mate. But she gave it to Marty.

I half expected Marty to laugh, or show it to Janet (whose eyes were bulging out of her head from craning to see), or wad it up and throw it back at me. Instead she stared at it for a long time, shielding it from Janet with her hand. Then she wrote something on the bottom, and passed it back. It said:

> Jules,
> Yes, please!!! I've really missed you too. And I'm sorry I was so jealous, but you were so good at the audition and I was just T*E*R*R*I*B*L*E and I knew it! But I think it's really great that you're Lyra. I can hardly wait to see you in the play.
> Marty xxx
> P.S. All Janet ever talks about is Pony Club. BORING.

I looked over at Marty. We smiled at each other.

Chapter Eleven

I told her everything at break, my words spilling over themselves like a waterfall. All of it, every horrible little bit, right from the start.

'Oh, *Jules*,' breathed Marty. 'Poor you! Divorce . . .' She looked down at the half-eaten chocolate bar she was holding, and shuddered. I knew she was thinking about her own parents, who are so lovey-dovey and perfect that they're practically like another species. I swallowed, and stared over at the playing fields where some Year Tens were playing rugby.

'But it's not *always* such a terrible horrible thing,' said Marty quickly. 'Really. My aunt and uncle got divorced last year, and my cousin Sheila says it's loads better now. All they did was fight before, and she hated that. Just like you.'

'I know. It's not *that* so much. It's not knowing where Dad is, or why he won't ring me, or—' I blinked hard, and sniffed.

Marty's eyes were warm and worried. 'I know. It must be awful . . . Jules, I'm such a *louse!* All the time you were going through this, and I was just sulking and wasting time with *Janet*. You must hate me!'

'No, I thought *you* hated *me*.'

Her curls bounced about as she shook her head. 'I was just jealous. And stupid. I'm really, really sorry.'

'No, *I'm* sorry. I should have told you about all this, and not let you think I was lying to you.'

'Get real!' She pushed my arm. '*I'm* the one who should be sorry, not *you*.'

We burst out laughing. She offered me her chocolate bar, and I took a bite. 'But what about the blood test? Tell me the truth, OK? Do you think something's wrong with me?'

She pursed her lips. 'No,' she said finally.

'But why—'

'I don't know. But you're not ill, I'd bet on it. We'll find out what's going on, don't worry. We just need a plan of action.' Marty's eyes had narrowed to dark brown slits. She always used to want to be a detective. When we were eight, she used to wear a deerstalker and carry a magnifying glass around, and call me 'Watson' until I wanted to smack her.

She laughed suddenly, and licked a bit of chocolate off her fingers. 'Remember Sherlock and Watson?'

'Yup,' I grinned at her.

It was great to have my best friend back. Especially when we walked into the science building together, and Vicki and her lot saw us.

'Hanging out with Miss Star, are you, Marty?' called Vicki. 'Ooh, maybe we can get *your* autograph, too!' She nudged Janet, who was hanging about on the fringes of Vicki's gang. Janet giggled on cue, looking thrilled to be included.

We swanned past them, noses up. Marty tucked her arm through mine. 'You should have seen Vicki's face when she heard me talking about you getting the part of Lyra,' she whispered in my ear. 'She was even greener than *me*.'

Marty sat at the computer desk in the corner of Mum's bedroom, swivelling the red chair from side to side. The PC warmed up with little whirrs and hisses. 'I can't *believe* you haven't checked it out on the internet yet.'

I couldn't either, now that she had mentioned it, but I just shrugged. 'I hardly ever come in here anymore. Just to check my email, to see if Dad's written.' Which he never had. I shoved the thought away. 'It's *her* room. It makes me feel ill to even be in here.'

Marty shook her head briskly. 'It's the *information superhighway*, Jules! It's how you find things out in the twenty-first century!' The computer gave a final hum as it resigned itself to being awake. Marty clicked on to the icon for our internet server and started typing.

Five minutes later, our jaws hit the floor with a double *thud*. Because typing in 'blood test' under Websearch brought up 4,722 matches! We'd never get through them all, never. Not even if we sat here all night. Not even if we sat here until we had cobwebs attached to us.

'Wow,' said Marty.

I was too busy gaping at the first page of titles. 'Marty – look!'

Blood Test Measures Cell Damage From Radiation
Blood Test for Diabetes
New Blood Test Developed for Breast Cancer
Blood Test for Alzheimer's Disease

And on and on, scarier and scarier. Marty shook my arm. 'Jules! You don't have *any* of those!'

'How do you know? How?'

'Well, you can't have *breast* cancer, can you? You have to have *breasts* for that.' I scowled at her. She kept on: 'And Alzheimer's is for old people. So relax.'

'Yes, and what about diabetes, then? *Radiation?*'

'Not listening.' She clicked on to the next page.

Leukaemia. Chagas Disease. Toxic Hepatitis.

Even Marty gulped a bit at that last one. She clicked forward hurriedly. Spondylitis. Down's Syndrome. *Cancer.*

'Maybe . . . this wasn't a good idea,' she said weakly.

I dropped down on the bed and stared at the stark blue letters on the screen. 'Don't be stupid. It's a *wonderful* idea to find out that I have some sort of – *tumour* or something growing inside of me. Getting bigger and bigger, about to explode any second in a huge fountain of black goo, and—'

Marty tucked a curl behind her ear. 'Having hysterics will not solve anything,' she informed me. 'We need a plan. The first part of the plan is that you have to *talk to your mother*. If you *do* have something wrong with you, you deserve to know. Only I really don't think you do. I really don't, Jules!'

*

OK, Marty was right. I needed to talk to Mum. I kept putting it off though – I mean, my God – I had so much to worry about already that I practically needed a Worry Schedule to fit it all in, and what if something really *was* wrong with me? I didn't want to know, I really didn't. *Toxic hepatitis*?

So the rest of that week went by. And the start of the next. And every day Marty sprang at me and said, 'Have you asked her yet?' and then shook her head and groaned, *'Ju-ules,'* because I hadn't.

Finally, on Monday night I couldn't stand it anymore. After lying awake in bed for hours biting all my fingernails off one by one, I snuck downstairs and rung Uncle Derek again.

Crash, bang. 'Mmf? H'lo?'

'I'm *really, really* sorry to wake you up again.' I was twining the phone cord about my hand, I was so nervous. (I didn't have any more nails to bite off by then.)

'Jules,' he groaned. 'Darling, can't this wait—'

'No, it's a total emergency! There's something I've got to know.'

I heard him draw a quick breath. 'What?'

'When you had lunch with Mum last week, what did you talk about? Was it about me?'

Another pause, and then his voice changed. Most people probably couldn't even tell the difference, but I knew it right away: it was his *acting* voice.

'Yes, of course. Your mother is very concerned about the effect all of this might be having on you, you know. So am I, for that matter. But we didn't discuss you apart from that. Why do you ask?'

My stomach clenched as he spoke. He was lying to me. Uncle Derek was *lying*. I said slowly, 'Because I had to have a blood test, and – I've been worried that I have some sort of disease or something.'

I heard the soft sound of his breath relaxing, but it was still his acting voice as he said, 'Well, put your mind at ease, love. You're perfectly fine. And now, I'm sorry, but I have to get back to sleep. Early day tomorrow, you know.'

I was more worried after I hung up than I had been in the first place.

And then on Tuesday afternoon, the *next* weird thing happened.

I had forgotten my script for play practice, only of course I didn't realize it until we were halfway to the Flying Frog, so Mum had to turn the car around and take me home to get it. Then she popped inside the house too, to check her phone messages.

And as we left the house again about ten minutes later, this bloke in jeans and a denim jacket jumped out from behind a hedge and snapped our photo. *Flash*, right in our faces! I mean, *eh?*

We both stopped and stared at him. I thought he was a complete nutter, but Mum had gone chalk-coloured. 'You can't *do* that,' she gasped.

The man – he had a long brown ponytail – just laughed. 'Righteous indignation, very nice! Point it here, love.' He held up the camera again, at which point Mum ducked behind her hand and hustled me into the car. And as we squealed away from the kerb,

I could see him standing in the road, still snapping away. Taking pictures of our car.

A tight sickness filled my chest. '. . . Mum?'

She started gabbling away, staring at the road. 'There's a – court case at work, very high profile. The press is supposed to leave us alone, but they don't always, obviously. Nothing to worry about.' Her mouth clamped firmly shut.

I didn't ask any more. I was too scared. What had Mum *done?*

'Jules, where *are* you today?' called Diane after I fluffed my fourth line in about five minutes.

'Sorry.' I started the scene again. *Be Lyra!* Forget about Mum. You can ask her tonight what's going on. But when she picked me up that night, I took one look at her and knew I couldn't. Her lips were so stiff and sharp you could use them for scissors.

The next morning wasn't any better. I sat picking at toast and eggs, and watched Mum flip through the pages of the morning paper. She never reads the paper at breakfast. Now her fingers gripped the pages too tightly as she snapped through it, page after page.

Just ask. What can she do to you? Ask!

Suddenly Mum made a choking noise and went white. I jumped up. *'Mum?'*

Her eyes were scanning something in the paper, flying back and forth across the page. 'Mum, what *is* it?'

'Nothing.' She folded the paper up, fumbling and getting the creases all wrong. 'Sorry. Just – something startled me.' She finished her coffee in a quick gulp, and stood up, tucking the paper under her arm. 'I need to finish getting ready. We'll leave in about ten minutes, all right?' Without waiting for an answer she bolted upstairs, high heels clacking.

I cleared my breakfast stuff away slowly, thinking.

Nine minutes later, Mum reappeared without the paper. *Twelve* minutes later, I waited for her to start the car and begin manoeuvring it out of its parking place before I opened my bag and ploughed through it.

'Oh, no! I forgot my science book – just be a second.' I popped out of the car before she could say anything, unlocking the front door and shooting inside.

I galloped up the stairs and into Mum's room, plunging into a frenzied search. Where would she have put it? Under the bed, in the bin. The drawer of her bedside table! Nowhere, it was nowhere. Mum might be getting out of the car by now, coming after me – *her bathroom!*

The paper was in the bin beside the sink. I scooped it up, flipping through it wildly – and then I stopped, staring. On page seven, there was a crisp, neatly-cut hole in the top right-hand corner, where an article used to be.

The newsagent was a squat little building with a green door, two streets down from Highfield Secondary. Marty and I ran all the way there at break, burst into the shop still running and pounced on the piles of newspapers under the magazines.

The *Observer*, the *Telegraph*, the *Guardian* . . .

'It's not here!' I wailed.

'D'you have today's *Daily Post?*' panted Marty to the woman behind the counter. The woman shook her head. She had wiry grey hair, like steel wool. Wiry whiskers poking out of her chin.

'Not even *one?*' I begged.

'Sorry, sold out.'

'Not even one teeny little one that maybe you bought for yourself and you have in the back, that we could just *look* at?'

Her cardy bulged at the seams as she gave a wheezy laugh. 'Not me. I read the *Sun.*'

I thought of flinging Dad's favourite quote about 'the great unwashed' at her, but Marty pulled on my arm. 'We have to *go*, Jules; break will be over.'

We made it back to school with two minutes to spare – sneaking in through the side gate and trying to look dead casual, as though we just *happened* to be hanging around here in this completely remote corner. We started walking back to the science building, drifting along with the other groups heading inside.

I hugged my elbows against the cold. 'Marty, what if Mum's done something really bad, and that's why Dad left?'

Her eyes widened. 'Like what?'

'I don't know. I mean *really* bad, like stealing from her company. I mean, what if they put her in jail?' Which, OK, I've thought she deserved a hundred times since Dad left . . . but what if they actually *did* it? Would they put me in a home? Some horrible place for unwanted kids, where I'd have to sleep in a room with twenty other girls and never get second helpings of anything?

'I have to see that paper. I *have* to.'

Marty's mouth twisted in thought. 'Maybe the library? Do they have papers?'

So at lunchtime, we shoved our way through the streaming corridors, struggling against the tide like salmon – but when we got to the library Mr Patel just shook his head. The school didn't get the nationals; just the local Jameston paper. And no, *he* didn't have a copy of the *Daily Post*; he read the *Telegraph*. He liked its crossword.

Marty grabbed my arm as we left the building. 'I know! The *city* library. You don't have play practice today, do you?'

My heart jumped. 'No, it's Wednesday.'

Marty took out her mobile and handed it to me. 'Here, ring your mum. Then I'll ring mine. We can go after school; we'll catch the bus.'

Mum didn't want me to catch the bus. Well, obviously. I'd get kidnapped and sold into slavery, never to be seen again. She came and picked us up after school instead, and then spent the whole drive making excruciating small talk with Marty.

'How's your mother doing?' She peered in the rear-view mirror at us.

'She's all right,' said Marty.

'Is she still teaching those classes? She's an artist or something, isn't she?'

'Embroidery.'

'Oh, yes, of course. Embroidery. Lovely.'

God! I slid down in my seat, mortified. I mean, *really*.

When we finally, after many painful centuries, pulled up in front of the library, Mum said, 'Maybe your mother would like to meet up for a coffee sometime. Tell her I'll ring her, all right?'

Marty nodded. 'Thanks for the lift, Mrs Cheney.'

I was out of the car by then, desperate to escape.

'I'll pick you up at half five, Jules,' Mum called after me. I lifted my hand without looking back, already heading up the library stairs.

Marty caught up with me as Mum pulled away. 'What's up with you?'

'Are you *kidding*?'

Marty shrugged, and adjusted her bookbag strap. 'She was just trying to be nice.'

'Yeah, well. We'll see how *nice* she is when we see what she was hiding in the paper, won't we?' I shoved through the revolving door and led the way to the desk, where there was a massive queue of people returning their books. A woman scanned them in slowly, one by one, with something that looked like an electronic pencil. *Blip!* Thank you. *Blip!* Thank you. Argh! I stood shifting my weight about, tapping my feet.

'Will you *relax*?' hissed Marty.

Finally it was our turn. With my fingers crossed tightly below the desk, I said, 'Do you have a copy of today's *Daily Post*?'

The librarian's eyebrows lifted. Probably because I

blurted it out like David Weedy Tallis asking Marty for the maths assignment.

'No, I'm afraid we don't. We have *old* issues of the *Daily Post* on microfiche, if that helps.'

'Oh.' I felt totally flattened, like someone had just run over me with a steamroller. Marty squeezed my arm.

The librarian frowned, obviously perplexed as to why not having the *Post* was such a catastrophe. 'Is Tesco out of them, then?' She saw from our faces that we didn't have a clue what she was on about. Reaching past us for the next customer's books, she said, 'There's a Tesco across the road. Try there, *they* sell papers.'

Five minutes later we were standing in the newsagent's section of Tesco, hunched over the last copy of the *Post*.

'Oh, *Jules*.' Marty breathed my name in soft horror.

I couldn't say anything. The article stabbed me in the stomach as I read it, each word like a shiny dagger cutting me to bits.

Chapter Twelve

Marty and I sat together on the library steps. She had her arm around my shoulders, and kept saying reassuring things like, 'No-one will know, *really*. I could hardly even tell it was you, I promise.' Only they weren't that reassuring. And she kept well away from mentioning the article itself.

There wasn't much reassuring that she could say about the article.

'No-one reads the *Daily Post* anyway!' Marty's voice sounded a bit desperate by now. 'No-one's going to pay *any attention* to it. Jules, are you listening? Really, no-one will even see it!'

I didn't answer. My throat felt like it would crumble to bits if I tried to talk. Finally, Marty's mum pulled up in front of the library. Marty waved at her and said, 'Do you want me to wait with you until your mum comes?'

I cleared my throat. 'No, it's OK.'

'I don't like leaving you alone.'

'It's really OK.'

Nothing would ever be OK again, ever, ever. And I

wished Marty would just go away, actually. She had her perfect parents, she could never understand how I felt. Except that was horrible of me – she was Marty, we had known each other forever, of *course* she understood.

I don't know what I felt. I just wanted to be alone.

Just then Mum drove up behind Marty's mum. I stood up. 'Are you OK?' asked Marty.

'Yes,' I lied.

'Ring me later, OK?'

I nodded and got in the car. And before Mum could say a word, I shoved the paper at her, folded back at the article. 'No wonder Dad left,' I said.

'Father' to sue over 'Child X'

A MAN is making legal history by suing his estranged wife for damages after tests proved he is not the father of their daughter.

The couple, who cannot be named because of a court order protecting Child X's identity, separated a month ago upon Mr X's discovery of the child's parentage, and are now divorcing.

Mr X located Farber Biotech, a company that specialize in paternity testing, over the internet and expressmailed hairs from Child X's hairbrush to them for DNA testing. A court-ordered blood test later confirmed the result of the American-based company.

Mr X is now suing Mrs X for 'deceit', the emotional distress caused by the discovery, and the costs, with interest, he incurred while bringing up Child X.

Mr X says he is 'devastated' by the discovery, and has had little contact with the child ever since. 'I can't bear looking at her and knowing the truth.'

When I first saw the article, I had just stood there in Tesco without moving, like a cardboard cutout of myself. Marty pressed beside me, reading over my arm. 'But that means your dad's not your dad!' she blurted out. Then she gasped and put her hand over her mouth. 'I mean – oh *Jules*—'

I hardly heard her. The words pummelled me as I read them over and over. Estranged wife. Deceit. They sounded horrible, like a swarm of bees. Like a chainsaw, chopping and tearing! I wanted to say, but this isn't about *us*. Except I knew it was. The blood test. Hairs from my hairbrush. I remembered finding my hairbrush moved that day I found all of Dad's stuff had gone.

I can't bear looking at her . . . But you're my dad! I shouted at him in my mind. I don't care what this says, you're my *dad*, how can you say that?

Almost worse that anything else was the photo. There we were, in stark grey and black: me and Mum leaving the house yesterday, Mum with her hand shielding her face. They had put black strips across our eyes so you couldn't tell it was us. Great disguise. It still looked *exactly* like me and Mum. You could even see the 'Che' of the painted sign on our house, 'The Cheneys'! 'Why, I wonder who that could be? The house looks familiar, but oh, I just can't place them, not with those super-disguising black strips in place!'

Under the photo, it said, 'DECEIT: *Mrs X attempts to hide while hurrying Child X, the innocent victim of the case, to the car.*'

Child X.

I folded the paper up carefully, and went to the check-out stand. 'You're not *buying* it, are you?' said

Marty, crowding along beside me. 'Jules, just leave it!'

I ignored her, and paid fifty pence. Marty grabbed at my arm. 'Jules, I *really* don't think it's good for you to have that. Just leave it here, put it back!'

I tucked the paper in my bookbag and zipped it up. 'It's *me*, isn't it?' I snapped.

Mum pulled a tissue from her handbag and wiped her eyes. The newspaper sat on the ledge over the glove box, shouting its horrible headline at us. 'I know it was wrong not to tell you. But I kept hoping he'd drop the case, and you wouldn't have to know . . .'

She had driven to Victory Gardens from the library, and now we sat in the car park with the windows misting up. I stared out the windscreen at the prickly winter cricket fields, my eyes granite-dry. A man with a lollopy-eared beagle walked past.

'What does it mean? What's "costs with interest"?' My voice sounded like it came from the bottom of a well.

Mum rubbed her temple, and said softly. 'It means . . . he's suing me because he's found out he's not your real father. And now he wants to be paid back all that he's ever spent on you over the years. Plus interest.'

I felt the colour leave my face. Dad wanted to be *paid* for being my dad? The world swam around me. I thought I was going to be sick. I gripped the door handle, ready to fling it open so I could decorate the tarmac.

Mum added hastily, 'Jules, he's very, very hurt, that's all. It's *me* he's trying to get at, really. He still loves you.'

Um. Well, he sort of has a funny way of showing it. Doesn't he? I swallowed, pushed down the sick feeling. I shoved at the newspaper, knocking it towards her. 'So who was he, then? My *real* father?'

Looking down, Mum shredded at the tissue, twisting a corner. 'No-one important. Just someone I went to university with, a boy I knew slightly. Jules, I don't expect you to understand. *I* don't even understand. It was a mistake. Your father and I had a fight before the wedding, and I made a terrible mistake . . .'

'Me, in other words,' I muttered. The beagle was chasing after a green rubber ball. Every time it barked, it seemed to stab through me, hurting me.

'No!' Mum reached over and cupped my face, stroking my cheek with her fingers. I'm not sure why, but I didn't pull away. A tiny tear escaped down my face. She dried it with a lock of my hair.

'Jules, I can't be sorry at all in *that* sense. You're wonderful, the best daughter ever. And – Ben loves you so much, sweetie. He'll get over this, I know he will.'

I can't bear looking at her.

I did pull away then, and suddenly I heard myself shouting, 'Why do they call me Child X? *Child X?* What's *that* supposed to mean? I have a *name*, why don't they use it?'

Mum swallowed. 'To spare you pain,' she whispered.

The next morning, I skulked about school like a timid mouse, not daring to look at anyone, positive that they all knew and were laughing at me. I could just hear Vicki and her lot crowing about it: 'Have you heard about Miss Star? She's so pathetic her dad wants to be *paid* for raising her!'

It didn't happen, though, and as the day went on I started to relax. Or could have done if it hadn't been for Marty. She had turned into superglue, plastered right to my side. She kept saying, 'Are you OK? Are you sure you're OK?' until I wanted to choke her.

OK, she was only trying to help, and I wouldn't know how to act if it were *her* parents either (not a chance) – but after a while it just made me feel about fifty times worse, the way she kept hanging about, looking so solemn and concerned. Like I really *did* have some flesh-rotting disease, and she was the only one brave enough to come near me.

So play practice that afternoon was a complete relief. No-one there knew that my father wanted his money back, so I could forget about it too, for a few hours.

'Right, let's do scene twelve,' called Diane from the second row.

All of us on stage went over to our places and got ready. Adrian and I clutched at each other's arms. I was too embarrassed to look him in the face while I did it. He didn't look at me, either. He hasn't for ages, not since that morning at school. In fact, practically the only time we say anything to each other is as Pan and Lyra.

He hasn't teased me any more since then, either.

Not that I care. I mean, really. As if I wanted to be called Brickface again.

Scene twelve is where Lyra's been captured, and the doctors are just about to cut through the invisible cord that links her to Pantalaimon. We've practised it loads of times now, and every time Diane's said the same thing: 'Good, Jules, but you could let yourself *go* a teensy bit more.' Which was extremely frustrating, because I always thought I had been.

But this time when the doctors advanced on Adrian and me, I stopped thinking altogether and just went berserk. I screamed and yelled and kicked and cried, but it was all right, it wasn't real. At the last moment, Lesley, as Mrs Coulter, rescued us, and relief swept over me as Adrian and I held on to each other, shaking. And then, escape! Other kids huddled together on the stage, and I shouted, 'Come with me! We've got to get out of the compound. Run!'

Nothing could touch me while I was Lyra.

'*Lovely*, Jules,' said Diane afterwards, beaming all across her freckled face. 'You've got it now; do it just like that from now on.'

I got home that night and stood in front of my bureau for a long time, looking down at the sapphire necklace in my jewellery box. It lay there winking at me, nestled against one of my plastic flower hair clips. Finally I picked it up, and let it slither from hand to hand, feeling its cool gold chain between my fingers and remembering when Dad gave it to me.

Then I went downstairs to the kitchen, quietly unlocked the back door, and threw it in the bin.

I left Eeyore on my bed, though. He looked so sad. It wasn't his fault.

I didn't know whose fault *anything* was any more.

It was mid-February by then. Still winter, still depressing. Occasionally a bit of watery sunlight would sneak through for an hour or so, but mostly it was just grey and miserable.

Exept at the Flying Frog. It was its own magic world there. That week, the set went up – a series of raised wooden platforms like giant wooden blocks, some of them really high, with sofas and chairs on the lower ones that could be made into all kinds of things. Plus we had been fitted for our costumes. I had a long-sleeved green tunic, belted at the waist over dark trousers, ancient and futuristic-looking at the same time. It was completely Lyra, and I loved it. The material itched though.

'Lovely! Hold it there.' *Snap, flash.* A photographer from the *Jameston Chronicle* had spent that whole Saturday morning herding us about from one side of the stage to the other, getting us to strike poses for him. Like I was really anxious to have my picture in the paper, *again.*

There was a reporter there, too. A woman with black hair and pink lipstick. 'Could I ask you a few questions about playing Lyra?' she asked me after the photos. 'I'm Lisa Vincent, by the way. Just call me Lisa.'

We sat down in the empty front row. She took a tiny tape recorder out of her saggy brown shoulder-bag and pressed the 'play' button.

'Right,' she said, smiling at me. 'Is this your first theatre experience?'

I nodded, and then realized it probably wouldn't record very well. 'Um, yes.'

'Diane Kosovich tells me that you're very talented. Do you plan to be an actress?'

'Yes, I do.' I looked down and played with a loose thread on my tunic.

The reporter – Lisa – asked me a few other questions, what I liked most about playing Lyra, and had I read the book the play was based on – and then suddenly she said, 'Juliet, is something wrong?'

'What?' I glanced up in alarm. Was it that obvious?!

Her slim shoulders lifted. 'You just seem a bit down for a girl who's starring in a play, that's all. Are you nervous about opening night?'

'Um . . . well, sort of, I guess.'

Lisa winced sympathetically. 'I can imagine. I'd be *terrified*, getting up on stage in front of all those people!'

I hesitated, plucking at the thread. 'It's not that, really. I just – well, I don't know if my parents are coming.'

'Oh, I see.'

'I mean, my dad. And . . . I really want him to.'

Her eyes were a soft, understanding greeny-grey. 'Yes, that would get me down, too. Why can't your dad come?'

'Well – he could, I guess. Only I don't know if he wants to.' I looked up at her again. She looked really nice. Concerned. 'My parents are getting a divorce,' I admitted.

'Oh, I *am* sorry,' said Lisa. 'I know just how you feel. My parents got divorced too, when I was about your age. Oh – here.' She clicked the tape recorder off, fumbling at the buttons a bit. 'Still trying to get used to this thing; it's new.' She tucked it away in her bag, and said, 'It's really rough, isn't it? Even if everyone keeps telling you it's for the best.'

She *did* understand! I nodded. 'Yes, exactly! Only it's not even the *divorce* so much – it's everything else that's happening, too. Like—' I stopped, not sure whether I ought to tell her *that*.

There was a pause, and then Lisa said, 'These things can get really messy, can't they? Everyone fighting for their rights, dragging solicitors into it. It's really sad when things turn out that way.' She kept her eyes on me, watching with a concerned frown.

'No – well, that's *sort* of it,' I said.

Lisa nodded and touched my arm. Her expression was so warm and encouraging, like she *totally* knew what I was going through. Then, I don't know – she was so nice that somehow I ended up telling her everything. About Dad suing Mum, and finding out that he's *not* my dad, and Child X, and all of it. And Lisa was completely great. She sat with her head propped on her hand, carefully following every word I said. And she asked all the right questions at just the right times, like she really understood and cared about how I felt.

I cried a tiny bit, but I don't think anyone noticed. Lisa passed me a tissue very discreetly.

Finally Diane came over and dropped her hands on my shoulders. 'Have you got enough now, Lisa? I'm afraid I need to steal Lyra back for rehearsal.'

Lisa nodded and stood up, swinging her bag over her shoulder. It gaped open, and she quickly clasped it. 'Yes, I think I've got enough, thanks.' She touched me on the head and smiled. 'It was lovely to talk to you, Juliet. Take care of yourself.'

Chapter Thirteen

I saw them from all the way across the courtyard on Monday morning – a huge group of Year Nines standing outside the art building. Twenty or thirty of them, maybe. Most of my group were there, and some others I didn't know very well, all of them huddled together in this big, jostling cluster.

I stopped in my tracks. And I was just telling myself not to be such a drama queen, that everything was perfectly OK and that they were probably just looking at some of those stupid alien trading-cards, when Marty ran up and grabbed my arm.

'Jules!' she panted. 'Jules, don't go through there – Vicki's reading it out loud—' She pulled me around the corner of the science building.

I jerked away. 'Reading *what?*'

Marty swallowed. '. . . Vicki's brought a paper in,' she said finally. 'It, um – has this long story about you in it. Jules, did you talk to a *reporter* on Saturday? It says you did, but—' She stared at me, looking pale and sick and excited, all at the same time.

Was *that* what everyone was so mesmerized by? I

tried to laugh, but only a sort of gasp came out. 'Marty, that's just the *Jameston Chronicle*. It's about the *play*.'

She slowly shook her head. 'No . . . Jules, it's the *Daily Post*. And it's about you: about Child X. There's a photo of you on stage . . .'

The world dropped away from me – *ka-thud*. My mouth opened. Nothing came out. I spun around and ran to the art building, my bookbag bouncing heavily against my shoulder.

'Jules, *wait!*' called Marty behind me. But I was already shoving my way into the group, ducking under arms to get to the centre of it.

Vicki was holding a newspaper, reading aloud. As I heard what she was reading, I turned to ice.

On a distant planet somewhere, I realized that Marty had followed me. And that nearly everyone around us was melting away, not looking at me.

Vicki raised her voice as she kept on:

'*Although the adults around Child X seem determined that the controversial court case should not affect her life, they are too late. The intelligent, talented young actress is all too aware of what is going on, and is clearly distraught by her starring role in the family tragedy—*'

I came to life all at once. 'Give me that!' I tried to rip it from her hands, but she held it out of my reach. 'Give it to me *now!*'

Vicki laughed. As I scrambled and clawed at her, she looked over at Georgina and Janet, and made an ''ooo, hark at *her*,' face. 'Did your dad not teach you to be *polite*, then? Oh, sorry – he's *not* your dad, is he?'

Marty, who's almost as tall as Vicki, dived in then, pushing at her and grabbing the paper. 'C'mon, Jules.' She put her arm around me and led me away. Behind us, I could hear Vicki and her lot giggling and snorting.

'Serves her right, stuck-up little thing.'

'No, don't be horrid! She's *intelligent and talented. Everyone* knows that!'

CHILD X SPEAKS OUT trumpeted the headline in the *Daily Post*. *'All I want is my dad back, says anguished Child X.'*

The story was all over the front page. And most of page two inside. There was even an *editorial* about it on page thirty-seven. I sat huddled up in the girls' loos reading, feeling cold and nauseous. *Naked.*

'When asked which parent she was most angry at, Child X considered the question carefully, obviously trying not to cry. "I don't know," she said finally. "I mean, I'm angry at Mum. I'm furious with her! But that's because of what she did to Dad fourteen years ago, before I was even born. And with Dad, it's for what he's doing to me now."'

Everything I had told Lisa, every single private feeling that I trusted her with, was there in print in a *national paper* for the entire world to see. There was even a photo of me on stage dressed as Lyra. And OK, they had done something to it so that all you could make out was this grainy figure with long hair – but you could still see the big wooden flying frog hanging from the ceiling! No wonder everyone knew it was me. It was totally *obvious*.

How could Lisa have *done* this to me? Maybe it was a mistake, maybe it was written by someone else. But even as I thought that, I knew how daft it was. Oh, right, someone else who just happened to put their name on it: BY LISA VINCENT. And besides, the story was crammed full of puke-making, *detailed* stuff like, *Child X is a graceful, small-boned teenager, with a vivacious expression that even the heavy weight of her current sorrow cannot wholly erase.*

I hated her. I hated her with every molecule of my existence. I hated her almost as much as I hated Vicki.

The first bell rang.

'I can't go to class,' I said to Marty. She was sitting in the stall with me, perched up on the water tank. 'Not with Vicki and everyone else knowing. I *can't!*'

Marty nibbled the side of her finger, which is what she always does when she's upset. 'What are you going to do, then? You can't hide in *here* all day.'

'Why not?'

'You just can't.'

I sniffed, and wiped at my eyes. I started folding up the paper, which wasn't easy since it was so crumpled.

'You should go tell Mrs Greaves what's happened,' said Marty. 'I bet she'd let you go home.'

'No, I don't want to.'

'Jules, you *can't* stay in here!'

I don't know why this set me off – the thought that

I couldn't stay in the grotty old loo all day – but it did, and I really started crying. I was still trying to fold the paper, making a right mess of it.

'I can't tell her!' I gasped. 'I just *can't*—'

Marty hopped off the water tank and crouched beside me, patting my arm. '*I'll* tell her. OK? Just come with me. It'll be all right.'

We went back and forth on this for about ten minutes, with me saying I can't, I can't, and Marty saying it would be all right, *really* it would. Eventually she managed to coax me out of the stall. Then we spent about ten *more* minutes with me splashing cold water on my face and then bursting into fresh salty tears again every time I saw how horrible and swollen my eyes and nose were, until finally Marty wouldn't let me look in the mirror any more and dragged me out into the corridor.

We were just heading across the courtyard towards the back entrance of the main building, Marty with her arm tight around my shoulders so I couldn't bolt, when a prefect came up to us, looking flushed and important.

'Juliet Cheney? Mrs Greaves wants to see you, *immediately.*'

At first, I just sat there in one of the hard green chairs and cried.

Mrs Greaves – who's about Gran's age, I think, but with soft blonde-grey hair and a cosy voice – took one look at me and didn't ask me to talk. She handed me a box of tissues and turned to Marty, who plunged into telling her all about Vicki and the *Daily Post* and Child X. I couldn't see Mrs Greaves' face, because I was too busy sobbing into soggy tissues, but I could hear her saying things like, oh dear, and I'll certainly have a word with *her*, and Hmmm.

Marty finished up, 'So I think that maybe the best thing would be if Jules could just go home? She lives near here, I could walk her.'

I looked up, dabbing at my eyes. 'Yes, please,' I sniffed. 'I can't stay here, I can't go to class—'

Her blue eyes looked sympathetic behind her glasses, but Mrs Greaves shook her head. 'I'm afraid it's a bit more difficult than that. Martine, thank you for being such a good friend to Juliet. You did just the right thing, staying with her, but I'd like you to go back to class now. I need to have a private word.'

Marty and I looked at each other. She frowned, dead worried, and I felt my eyes widen. No! Don't abandon me!

'She'll be all right,' said Mrs Greaves. 'Go on now, dear. Get a late slip from Mrs Cole.'

Marty slowly got up and left, shutting the door behind her.

Mrs Greaves sighed and took her glasses off, laying them on top of a pile of papers. She had a copy of the *Daily Post* on her desk, too, I noticed. Great. It was *everywhere*.

'Good heavens,' she murmured. 'What a terrible thing for you to have to deal with, Juliet. But one thing I promise you – it is *not* going to be made more difficult for you by any student in this school. I'm going to have very strong words with Vicki. She won't be teasing you about this again.'

I swiped at my eyes. They wouldn't stop leaking.

'Thank you,' I muttered, though privately I doubted she could do much. Vicki's a total expert at getting away with murder.

'Now, then.' She glanced down at the slashing black headline on her desk. 'I've already had your mum on the phone; that's why I sent for you. We agree that home is the best place for you at the moment. I'm going to take you myself, right away. She's there waiting for you.'

This all sound so stupidly Secret Agent that I gaped at her. 'But—'

She pushed the paper away as she stood up. 'I'm afraid there's a bit of a . . . situation, Juliet.'

The photographers were everywhere, swarms of them. All around the outside of the school fence, hanging over it, pointing cameras at me.

'Child X, look here! Over here!' Bright white flashes bursting away like Guy Fawkes night – *snap, whirr, snapsnapsnap!*

'Don't look at them.' Mrs Greaves kept her arm around me as she steered me over to the faculty car park. But I couldn't help looking. It was unreal, like being a celebrity. One photographer had even climbed a *tree*, and was snapping away from there!

The bell rang, buzzing through the morning air. A few seconds later, Year Nines started spilling out of the building, opening crisp packets and cans of Coke.

Our morning break. It was only half ten.

'Here, over here!' *Snapsnapsnapsnap!*

Mrs Greaves opened her car door for me, glancing tensely over her shoulder at the photographers.

'Put your head down,' she said as I climbed in.

Instead, I stared over at the group of kids. They all looked so carefree, so *normal*. And then, like a row of dominoes falling down, I saw people start to notice what was going on around the fence – heads turning, fingers pointing. I slid down in my seat.

Mrs Greaves paused on her side of the car, half in. 'Get back!' she shouted to someone, sweeping her arm in the air. 'No-one is to speak to them!'

I peeked out. Vicki and her lot, standing in the car park halfway to the fence. Oh *no*, she *wouldn't!* Hello, Mr Photographer. I'm Vicki Young and I have just *so* much to tell you about Child X.

'Back!' called Mrs Greaves. Slowly, they turned and went back to the courtyard. Vicki looked over her shoulder and simpered at me. I jerked my gaze away, face scorching.

There were more photographers waiting at our house, hanging about outside like it was 10 Downing Street. I scooted down in my seat again as Mrs Greaves whizzed past them, not stopping.

'Right, we'll outsmart them somehow,' she growled. And it was horrible, but it was also so *ridiculous* that I almost started laughing. Crikey, I was in a James Bond film! All I needed were dark glasses and a cigarette.

Mrs Greaves drove all the way down our street,

and then up the next street, parking in front of the house that's behind ours. Are you ready for this? After getting out of the car and peering about like a pair of escaped convicts, we snuck through this total stranger's back garden, and then climbed over the short wall and crossed through ours, knocking on the back door for Mum to let us in. (Mrs Greaves! Climbing over a garden wall! Marty would *not* believe it when I told her.)

Mum peeked out the kitchen curtains and then flung the door open, pulling me into a tight hug.

'Jules! Mrs Greaves, thank you, thank you so much —'

Mrs Greaves murmured something about how glad she was to help, and if there were anything she could do – but obviously there wasn't, so she left. Using the front door this time. The photographers went mad. ('Mystery woman leaves house of Child X!')

That whole morning, the phone wouldn't stop ringing. I could hear Mum getting more and more hysterical as she paced about, shouting into the cordless extension. 'No, I don't have a comment! There's a court order in place, you're to leave us *alone!*'

I hovered near the door, sickly fascinated. If you stood right beside it, you could hear the photographers talking to each other.

'Miserable weather, eh? Could do with a coffee.'

'And me. I'll pop up to the high street and get us some, shall I?'

'Oh, ta, mate; brilliant. We'll give you a print if Child X pokes her nose out.'

It made it worse, somehow, that they were all so matey. Like having a bunch of *united* barbarians waiting to storm your castle.

I could practically hear the net curtains twitching, all up and down the street.

Mum put the phone down and dropped on to the settee, gripping her head. 'I can't *believe* this—' The phone rang again. She snapped it up. '*Hello?* Oh, *George* – thank God! It's a bloody madhouse . . . yes, yes *please*, get here as soon as you can.'

George Arens is Mum's solicitor – not the one she and Dad both had together, but her new one since all of this started. He turned up half an hour later, screeching to a stop in a shiny black car, striding straight through the photographers like they were pesky flies. (*Snapsnapsnap!* Comment, guv'nor? Are you a relative of Child X? Here, look this way!)

'Right, I've spoken to the editor of the *Daily Post*.' Mr Arens sat in our big blue chair and ran a hand over his head. Slicking back his hair. Which was funny since he hardly had any, but I didn't feel like laughing just then. I sat curled in the corner of the sofa, hugging a cushion to my chest.

'And?' Mum sat beside me, gripping a mug of coffee.

'They're standing behind the article.'

'What!' Mum's knuckles whitened. 'How can they? Jules thought she was talking to someone from the *Jameston Chronicle!* They used false pretences, they—'

Mr Arens shook his head. 'No, Lisa Vincent *is* with the Chronicle. But she also sells the odd freelance article, and it was in that capacity that she wrote up and sold Juliet's story to the *Daily Post*.'

I imagined hurling Lisa into a gaping pit, and then shovelling a ton of *Daily Posts* over her. I chewed my fingernail as Mr Arens kept talking:

'They say that Juliet knew she was talking to a reporter, that she told Lisa Vincent the Child X story of her own accord, and that she said several times that she wanted to be heard, that she felt lost in the middle of all this. Ms Vincent said that despite Juliet's age, she felt duty-bound to give her the voice she had asked for.'

My mouth fell open. Because I *had* said all that about wanting to be heard – but only because Lisa had got me going on it, with her so, so sympathetic questions! And now she was using it against me, twisting it about like I had *asked* to be all over the front page!

'But what about the court order?' Mum fairly shrieked. She banged her coffee mug down on the table, splattering little brown drops. 'She's only thirteen, it doesn't *matter* what she said! They're not allowed to—'

Mr Arens pursed his lips together. 'You're right, of course, and the judge will undoubtedly charge them with contempt. But my impression is that this is what they want: for it to become a test case. How far can the press go when a child's identity is withheld? Because they haven't revealed Juliet's name or identity. She's still Child X as far as the British public is concerned – but they're pushing at the boundaries of what that means, hoping to have gained a bit of ground once the skirmish is over. The public's right to know, and all that.'

Still hugging the cushion, I finished nibbling off one nail and started on the next. Erm, excuse me, but why does the British public want to know what I look like with a black strip across my face?

Mum clutched at her head. 'And now we've got all the other tabloids jumping on the bandwagon, hounding Jules at *school*—'

'They're not on school grounds. Which is what they'll argue. Haven't they a perfect right to take photos of a public secondary school if they wish? Et cetera, and so on.'

Mum looked at me, her eyes brimming. 'Oh, Jules —'

I dropped my hand and hugged my elbows, squeezing the cushion about the middle. 'She seemed so nice,' I whispered. 'I didn't think she was going to publish it. She – she turned off her tape recorder when I started telling her about it—'

Mr Arens took a swallow of coffee, and put his mug on the table next to Mum's. 'She probably just hit the pause button, then released it.'

Two high spots of red appeared on Mum's cheeks. 'We'll fight it. We'll sue them.'

'Oh, you'd undoubtedly win,' said Mr Arens calmly. 'But you'd be fighting some very big businesses. It would take at least a year, and that's being optimistic.'

A year? Cold, wrenching panic swept over me. I dropped the cushion; it fell on the floor as I grabbed Mum's arm. 'Mum, no! Mum, please, I don't want to be Child X for a whole year, I *don't!* Please don't sue them, please—'

'All right, all right. Shhh, darling, don't worry.' Mum pressed me to her, rocked me. I nestled tightly against her, my heart thudding. I don't want to be Child X, I hate being Child X!

Mum stroked my hair. 'George, Jules is right. I can't put her through that – we'll just have to hope that all of this dies down as quickly as possible.'

Mr Arens' eyebrows quirked. He smiled sadly. 'Yes, fingers crossed. But you're an awfully big story, you know.'

Chapter Fourteen

The next day was like a weird sort of holiday: *Child X Day*, traditionally celebrated by staying home from school and hiding from photographers. They were all still hanging about, like there was a cocktail party outside our house. One of them had even brought doughnuts.

I raised an eyebrow as Mum put on a huge pair of dark sunglasses. Inside the house.

She took a deep breath. 'Right, here goes.' She opened the door with an arm flung over her face like Dracula meeting daylight, fumbled for the papers as a scurry of snaps went off, and then lunged back inside.

'Uh, Mum . . .?'

'What?' She pushed the sunglasses back up her nose, sifting through the teetering pile of papers. 'I didn't want them to get my face. Here, take some of these.' She handed me *The Times* and the *Guardian*.

'OK . . . but why are you wearing sunglasses? The photos put black strips across your eyes anyway.'

Mum stared at me, her eyes barely visible through

the smoky lenses. 'Ah.' She took the glasses off and smiled sheepishly. 'Never mind. Next time I'll wear a bag over my head, eh?'

We spread the papers across the dining table, like a black and white tablecloth. Mum had got all the major papers, and they all screamed the same thing:

A CHILD BETRAYED: *The innocent victim in the Child X case*

PATERNITY RIGHTS HIGHLIGHTED IN CHILD X CASE

DAILY POST ARTICLE SPARKS CONTROVERSY: Child X solicitor 'considering legal action'.

It was amazing. It was horrible.

And between the *Daily Post* and the *Clarion* there was an entire album's worth of photos. The life and times of the 'Black-Strip-Across-The-Eyes' family. Me walking beside Mrs Greaves; me getting into Mrs Greaves' car. Mum with her head down, going in our front door.

There was even one of Dad, getting off his motorcycle in front of an unfamiliar house. I stared at that one for ages. And the longer I did, the more I felt like boiling lava was blistering through my veins.

He looked so *bland*, like, ho hum, getting off my bike. Didn't he *care*? He had told the whole country that he wanted his money back, that he couldn't bear to look at me – and look at him, so relaxed and casual, pulling off his helmet!

I wanted to rip the photo out, tear it to shreds. *Obliterate* it. And at the same time, part of me wanted to get the scissors and cut it out carefully and tuck it away in a scrapbook or something, because it was Dad . . .

Mum cleared her throat. I glanced up to see her dark eyes filled with worry, watching me. She touched my arm. 'Jules . . . I'm so sorry that you have to go through this. It's not *your* fault.'

I looked down at Dad on his bike.

'Sweetie, you don't think it *is* your fault, do you?' Mum leaned over in her chair to put her arm around me.

'No . . .' The photo wavered. Because maybe he would have stayed, maybe he could have *overlooked* the fact that I wasn't really his daughter if I had been better or something. I don't know. I knew it was probably stupid, but I did sort of wonder about it.

'It's not,' said Mum firmly, squeezing my shoulders. 'It's mine. Blame me all you like, but don't blame yourself. Ever.'

I shrugged and leaned away from her a bit. She took the hint and dropped her arm. Lighting a cigarette, she said, 'Right . . . now, what should we do about school?'

Relief, something else to think about. I stood up and stacked all the papers into a big pile, shoving them down to the end of the table. 'What do you mean?'

Mum waved her cigarette at the front room, which sat draped in gloomy darkness. We didn't dare open the curtains, with the barbarians clustered outside. 'Well, you see what it's like . . . maybe it's best if you stay home until this is over. I could pick up your assignments for you. What do you think?'

I almost shouted, Great idea! But then I thought, if I don't go to school, she won't let me go to play practice, either. *I'd have to give up Lyra.*

'No, I want to go back to school!' I stood gripping the table, bouncing a bit on my toes, I was so nervous. 'And to play practice.'

Mum took a drag on her cigarette and didn't say anything. My hands tightened on the table edge. I was suddenly woozy with fear that she'd say absolutely not, that she'd take Lyra away from me. *'Please?'* I squeaked.

She exhaled a stream of smoke. 'If it's that important to you . . . I suppose it's good for you to stay in your routine if we can manage it. I'll have a word with Mrs Greaves and see what she says.'

I relaxed then, because I knew Mrs Greaves would tell Mum to get me back to school pronto, Child X or not. As if a head would really let you stay away in your SATS year! Unless you were dying, and maybe not even then.

Mum sighed, and rubbed her neck. 'But you realize we'll probably have to ask Granny Sophie to stay in that case.'

'Why?' I sank back down again, and pulled a knee to my chest.

She took another puff, tapped a crumbling stick of

ash onto her saucer. 'Because you'll have to have an adult with you at all times, escorting you to school and play practice. And I rather think I'm going to be tied up for a while.'

So Granny Sophie moved in. She didn't waste any time about it, either – she showed up that same night, dragging two bulging brown suitcases with designer symbols splashed all over them.

Mum's face crumpled. 'Oh Sophie, I'm so sorry about all of this—'

Gran hugged her briskly, almost pushing her away at the same time. 'Yes, well. I don't condone what's happened, but it's in the past, isn't it? Right now, *Juliet* is the important thing – though I think my son has forgotten that. Have you heard from him? I don't even know where he *is*.'

Mum groped at her jumper sleeve for a tissue. She blew her nose and said, 'Staying with one of his friends in London, I assume. I don't really know; I've only heard from him through his solicitor. But the preliminary hearing is tomorrow. I'll see him in court then.'

'I didn't know that!' I blurted from the lounge doorway. 'What does that mean, preliminary hearing? Can I go with you?'

Mum looked tired. 'No, Jules, of course not. You're going back to school, remember? And it's the hearing to see whether or not the court case should go ahead.'

My heart flew up. 'You mean it might *not*?'

'It depends on what the judge says.'

I opened my mouth to argue about not going with her, and then looked away, tracing a pattern on the wallpaper with my finger. Maybe I didn't want to see Dad after all. He'd be there arguing that the case *should* go ahead, that he should get paid back for every Mars bar he ever bought me plus interest.

I don't care. I hope he gets shedloads of dosh if that's what he wants, and that then he zooms off a cliff on his stupid motorcycle. I think *I* should get some money, actually, for having to have him as a dad all these years.

As though she could read my thoughts, Gran came over and hugged me, wrapping me in a rich cloud of perfume. 'Never mind,' she said. 'Never mind.'

I lay in bed that night thinking about the court case. How expensive had raising me been? Did Dad want to be paid back for *everything*? Did he have a list? Food and clothes and holidays? Christmas presents? Maybe he'd take off presents I'd given *him* – like the Harley-Davidson T-shirt I gave him last Christmas against the sapphire necklace he gave me, so that Mum only actually owed him twenty quid or something for it.

The lava started boiling again as I thought of the T-shirt. I had gone to so much trouble over it, even ordering it from a special shop in London. How could I have been so *thick*? He didn't care anything about me at all. He just cared about DNA tests and blood types. Dropping me like a load of rubbish, acting like I had tricked him or something, like it was all my fault.

Well, now I knew what he was *really* like. Who

needed him, anyway? I was glad he had buggered off. I burrowed under the duvet, wrapping myself up tightly.

Mum rapped on my door. 'Jules, could I talk to you for a minute?'

I said OK, and she came in and turned my desk light on. But at first she didn't talk at all. She just stood there looking down at my school papers, looking like a waif in her big green dressing-gown.

'What is it?' I sat up in bed.

'You didn't tell me you were starring in the play,' she said softly.

My stomach sank like the *Titanic*. How stupid could you get! Of course she knew; the *Daily Post* article had gone on and on about it. 'Um – I—'

Mum sat down beside me on the bed and touched my hair, brushing a strand away from my face. 'It's all right. I understand if . . . I mean, I'm proud of you, Jules.'

At half seven the next morning, Mum came downstairs wearing a dark blue suit, teetering on her heels like she had forgotten how to wear them.

She posed for me. 'All right?'

Yes, lovely, just the thing for that special court appearance. I lifted a shoulder, not wanting to think about why she was getting dressed up. Mum glanced in the hall mirror and patted her lipstick with a tissue, then picked up her briefcase and sighed, looking at the front door like there was a pack of lions on the other side.

'Better go out the back, I guess.'

The garden wall! I followed her into the kitchen. Gran was in there, making a pot of tea. Mum peeked through the kitchen curtains. 'Right, the coast is clear, I think.'

From the kitchen window, I watched her struggle across the garden wall in her suit – hefting herself up to sit on it and then swinging her legs about and hopping down the other side. Then she stood in the neighbour's back garden for a few seconds, brushing her bum off.

They must think we're completely demented.

Naturally, *Gran* was not about to climb over any garden wall. So half an hour later, the photographers pounced on us as soon as we opened the door, springing forward like we had jerked them on a chain.

Click, snap, flash! 'Grandma! Look this way! Child X, over here!' Gran looked like she was about to start whacking away at them with her long black brolly, but instead she just pressed her lips together and hustled me along to her car with her fingernails digging into my arm.

More photographers waited at the school gates. I slid right down in the seat so they couldn't see me, but I heard them snapping away. Gran parked the car in front of the school, even though you're not supposed to stop in the drive there, and walked me up the front steps.

A growing cluster of uniforms pressed against the windows inside, watching. Kids being dropped off climbed slowly out of their cars, staring at me.

'Gran, you can leave now!' I hissed. 'Everyone's looking.'

'Not until you get inside the building,' she said grimly.

Mrs Greaves appeared, pressing through the throng of students. 'Remember what I told you now,' she barked. Everyone scurried away. She held an arm out to me as I walked towards the door.

'Thank you, Mrs Cheney. It's a bit awkward, all this, but I'm sure it's the right thing to keep Juliet in school. We'll work around it, somehow.'

The changing of the guard. Gran left and now Mrs Greaves took over, shepherding me down the corridor. 'I've discussed with your mother the best way to handle this, and we've agreed that as far as possible, you should just carry on as normal.'

Normal. With photographers waiting to snap me, and the head escorting me down the corridor like I was a visiting popstar. As we walked through the building, people looked quickly away when they saw me, and then gaped once my back was turned. No, I'm not being paranoid – I could *feel* it. My back grew stiff, deflecting all the stares.

'Most of your classes are around the inner court-yard, so they can't bother you there. For lunch and your break, though, it's probably best if you go to the library, so you don't have to cross over to the west side of the campus. You brought your lunch today, didn't you? Yes, good. And if you're doing anything in the playing fields for PE, the library is probably best then, as well.'

Why don't I just hide in there all day, like a mole? 'Can Marty eat in the library, too?' I said in a small voice.

'Who?'

'Martine Fulson.'

'Oh, Martine. Yes, I think so.' She gave me a hearty smile, like this was all just a big jolly adventure.

I didn't smile back. 'You're not going to walk me to all my classes, are you?' We were almost to the art building and I could see Vicki and her gang hanging about the doorway, watching.

Mrs Greaves saw them, too. 'No, I'm sure that's not necessary. I've told everybody how I expect them to behave, so you shouldn't have any trouble. But if you do,' she gave Vicki a hard look, 'then I want you to come straight to me. Do you understand?'

'Yes. Thank you,' I muttered. Told *everybody*? My chest clenched.

The moment she turned away, I dashed past Vicki into the building. She shoved me with her shoulder as I passed. '*Ex*-cellent to have you back, X.' Titter titter, ho ho.

Inside, Marty was talking to David Weedy Tallis, both of them leaning against one of the art display cabinets.

'Jules!' Her face lit up when she saw me, and she waved me over. 'We didn't think you'd come! What's been *happening*? I kept trying your line yesterday, and it was busy—'

'We took it off the hook after a while.' I gave David a sideways scowl. *Go away.*

Red swept his cheeks. He straightened up off the cabinet. 'Well, um, I'll see you later, Marty. Bye, Jules.' He ambled off.

'*Jules!*' Marty swatted my arm. 'What did you do *that* for?'

'Because I have to talk to you!' I told her about Mrs Greaves. 'Marty, what did she mean? Told *everybody*?'

Marty started to answer, and then looked at the door. 'Uh oh,' she murmured. I followed her gaze and saw Vicki and the others, heading right for us. I squared my shoulders and watched them come, trying to look braver than I felt.

They passed slowly by, sort of swaggering, giving me sidelong glances. Someone hissed, 'Why are we supposed to be nice to her? I bet Miss Star *loves* having all the photographers around!' And they all cackled, but at least they kept on going down the corridor. I relaxed, slumping against the display case. Some lumpy seventh-year pottery rattled inside.

Marty's face had turned sombre. 'That's what I was trying to ring you about. Mrs Greaves held a special assembly about you yesterday morning. The entire school was there.'

'Oh, *no*,' I breathed.

'She didn't say your name or anything, but she said one of the Highfield Secondary students was going through a terrible family crisis that was in the press, and we were all to be very supportive of your privacy – well, she didn't say it was you, but everyone *knew*, you know—'

I knew.

'And that nobody was to say *anything* to any reporters or photographers. And she went on for a really long time about how we all had to be caring and understanding and put ourselves in your place and all that.'

I winced, picturing it. How completely *painful*. How could Mrs Greaves humiliate me like that? Fine, OK, she meant well in her fuddy-duddy way, but she didn't have a single clue! Telling the *entire school* to be nice to poor Jules, as if that was supposed to make things easier for me!

The bell rang. In a daze, I followed Marty into the classroom. And it was like a gargoyle had walked in. Everyone stiffened and looked awkwardly away when they saw me. One of two offered a nervous, sickly smile before diving into their exercise books. Vicki snickered, and whispered something to Janet.

Thank you so much, Dad.

Chapter Fifteen

Gran was waiting for me after school. She walked me back *down* the steps again, like I was a thick six-year-old. I could see the photographers frothing at the fence, jostling to get a good view as I got in the car. I slithered way down in the seat, and we drove past them in a blur of flash bulbs and shouts.

'Child X! Look this way!'

'Over here!'

Would everyone at play practice be huddled in little groups reading CHILD X stories, whispering and laughing? Maybe Lisa Vincent had ruined the Flying Frog for me, too, so that having to go there and be Lyra would be *horrible* now. The thought made my stomach ache.

I relaxed a bit once we got to the theatre. There was just the carpark, and the same row of shops and buildings as usual. No ravaging hordes of camera-wavers, waiting to pounce.

Except that once we got out of the car, I heard a shout: 'Child X!' My head swivelled about automatically. Two of them, standing around the side of the theatre. *Snapsnapsnapsnapsnap!*

And then I saw Mike, the boy who played Lord Asriel, heading towards the theatre doors. One of the photographers beckoned to him. 'Here, do you know Child X?' Mike stopped and walked over to them.

I stared at him, totally stricken, with Gran pulling at my arm and hissing, 'Come *along*, Juliet, or we'll get back in the car this instant!' I looked over my shoulder as she dragged me away. Mike was standing there talking to them.

When Diane saw us enter the lobby, a strange expression came over her face. She hurried over to us, and at first I don't know what I thought – that maybe she was going to tell me to go away, that I had caused her enough trouble already – but instead she hugged me.

'Jules, I'm so sorry about everything. I feel like it's my fault—'

'Don't be silly,' snapped Gran. 'It's *Lisa Vincent's* fault. I'm Sophie Cheney, by the way – Juliet's grandmother.'

She said it with no hesitation at all, but it suddenly hit me – if all this is true – I mean, it *is* true – then she's not my grandmother, is she? The mother of some bloke Mum knew at university is *really* my granny. Sitting in some innocent semi-detached somewhere, drinking tea and never even suspecting about me. No, that's too weird, I can't think about it.

Diane shook her hand, and told Gran that she didn't need to worry about the press *here* – that she was going to lock the front doors once everyone in the cast had turned up, and only leave the side fire doors open during rehearsal.

'And I can see both of them from the third row, which is where I sit. Believe me, Mrs Cheney, I know what the press is capable of, and *nobody* will get in here without my knowledge.'

Gran nodded. 'I'm very glad to hear it. Would you mind, though, if I stayed for rehearsal tonight? I'd very much like to see Juliet's acting.'

Diane smiled and said of course. My eyebrows flew up as I looked at Gran. She's never said a *single word* about my acting before! She didn't now, either. She just gazed calmly back at me, chin up.

Mike walked in. I looked away, flushing, hating him for talking to those people – but he came right up to us, a scowl heavy across his face. 'Diane, did you know that some prats from the press are out there? They're trying to talk to people going in.'

'Not for long.' Diane strode out of the theatre like a commando. Gran frowned and followed her, watching out the door.

I managed to look at Mike. 'Did one of them talk to *you?*' I accused.

'Yeah.' Mike grinned at me. 'I gave him a real exclusive – said my name was Lord Asriel, and that you were my secret love child with Mrs Coulter. Reckon that'll be front page in the *Post* tomorrow.'

His face sobered at my expression. He put a hand on my shoulder. 'Jules, don't be stupid. I told him to go to hell. That's what *any* of us would say to one of them. Don't worry, all right?' He winked at me and put on an American gangster voice: 'You're aces with us, sweetheart.'

Adrian and I stood in the wings, waiting for our cue.

'Jules?' he whispered.

He hadn't spoken to me since That Time. An embarrassed flush lit my cheeks as I looked at him. 'What?'

His brown eyes were almost black in the dim backstage light. 'I just – I wanted to tell you that I'm really sorry about . . .' He saw my face stiffen and trailed off. 'Well, about Vicki, and all that.'

All that. I bit my lip and nodded. Oh, please don't be nice to me, not after I was so completely horrible to you! It was almost time for us to go on. Adrian glanced at the stage, and saw that it was, too.

'And – listen, Jules?' He spoke all in a rush, his words tumbling over each other: 'I didn't think you'd come tonight. But – I'm really glad you did.'

Then we were Lyra and Pan again, warily entering Lord Asriel's lair.

'Feeling refreshed?'

Mike lounged on the leather sofa. Therese, the thin blonde girl who plays his snow-leopard daemon, sat curled beside him.

'Yes, thanks.' I sat down in the chair opposite him. The stage lights warmed my face. Adrian crouched at my feet, and pretended to nervously groom his whiskers.

'So, Lyra, tell me . . . how does John Faa come into this?' Mike narrowed his eyes, and I glared back at him. This was Lord Asriel. My father.

And I was furious with him.

'First you have to tell *me* something. Are you my father?'

Mike yawned. 'Yes. So what?'

I didn't think about staging at all, I just sprang to my feet because it was natural to, and cried, 'You should have told me before, that's so what! Why didn't you? What difference would it make if I knew? I'd have been so proud – but you never! You told other people, but never me!'

Real life crashed through like a tidal wave, and I was talking to Dad. Maybe the speech didn't make sense so far as he was concerned, but Dad was still the one I was shouting at.

'You ain't human, Lord Asriel,' I spat. 'You ain't my *father!* Fathers are supposed to love their daughters.'

Granny Sophie hardly said a word on the way home from rehearsal.

'My heavens, you're talented,' she murmured. Her eyes looked far away as she shifted gear, like she was thinking of something else completely.

But she meant it, I could tell, and it gave me a nice warm feeling inside. 'Thanks, Gran,' I said shyly.

And then she said something sort of strange. 'I wonder how your Uncle Derek is doing.' She cleared her throat. 'I mean, with taping his series.'

Mum was waiting for us when we got home. She was still wearing her dark blue suit, only now it looked creased and wilted.

She cleared her throat. 'I have something to tell you both.' But it was me she was looking at. 'The hearing decided that the court case should go ahead.'

The next few weeks passed in a total blur, with photographers rustling in our front shrubbery, and popping out from behind our car, and hiding in the fridge, teeth chattering, ready to spring out at us the second we opened the door.

OK, not that last one. But I bet they would have done if they could have squashed into it. They were everywhere *else*. Hanging about the school fence. Lurking in the doorway of the tandoori place across the road from the Flying Frog. Plus now there were usually reporters, too, shouting out questions as I passed:

'Child X, have you heard from your dad yet?'

'How do you feel about the court case, Child X?'

In the newspapers, in magazines, on television – all that you could see or hear *anywhere* was Child X.

'*Welcome to* Frontline. *Tonight, our panel will discuss the controversial Child X case, where a man is suing his estranged wife—*'

CHILD X: A MOTHER'S BLAME, A FATHER'S SHAME. '*It's terrible, I just feel so sorry for the poor little thing,*' said a neighbour yesterday . . .

'. . . allegedly the first court-protected teenager to independently grant an interview to the press, though lawyers for Child X say that the interview was not sanctioned, and that they are considering whether to press charges . . .'

BBC2 – CHILD X: THE PATERNITY QUESTION. *What makes a father? On the back of the controversial Child X case, four men tonight discuss their feelings of anguish upon discovering they are not the fathers of their children . . .*

BRAVE CHILD X CARRIES ON AS USUAL. *Child X, shown here arriving at school, makes a valiant effort to keep to her normal routine despite her family tragedy.*

It was unreal. It was like being in a play all the *time*, one I hated but couldn't get out of. I usually walked staring at my feet, with red slowly creeping across my face like glowing coals.

'Child X, look this way!'

Snapsnapsnapsnap!

'Degenerates!' snapped Gran once, steering me to the car.

'Just doin' our job, Grandma,' one of them called back.

Why hadn't they run out of film yet? Why couldn't they go take pictures of a *war* or something?

Marty said that all the secretaries and everyone at her dad's office were always talking about it, watching all the TV specials and clucking over the

Daily Post every morning. 'Oh, it's just dreadful. Oh, that poor child.' Marty's dad doesn't let on that he knows me, she says. He's afraid they'd all come stampeding to my doorstep and snatch me away and take me home with them, like I was a stray puppy.

I think it was even worse for Mum. I couldn't sleep one night, so I went downstairs to make myself some hot chocolate. And I found her sitting on the settee in the dark. At first she really scared me, because all I saw was a *shadow*. But once I edged into the room, I could see her sitting there, curled up with her legs under her.

'Mum?'

She started. 'Oh – Jules.'

'Are you all right?' I snapped the lamp on, and she winced at the sudden bright circle of light. 'Yes, I suppose. It's just—' She nodded at a paper on the coffee table. 'It's getting to be a bit wearing.'

The paper was folded open to yet another Child X article, this one on Mum. It had a big photo of her coming out of the courtroom with her eyes blacked out. **'LIED:** *Mrs X, who deceived her husband for years, leaves the courtroom upon finding out that the controversial court case will go ahead.'*

Mum smiled wryly. 'My co-workers know it's me now. The press has started ringing the office, fishing about, asking if I was cheating on Ben all along. If I had any boyfriends. My *boss* rang to tell me this.'

I perched on the edge of the settee. 'Will you lose your job?' I whispered. I wanted her to say, no, of course not, don't be silly.

Instead she just sighed, and rubbed her forehead. 'I

hope not. It's fairly humiliating, either way. I don't understand how Ben could do this to us. I know he's hurt, but . . .' She shook her head.

'Mum, would you . . . like some hot chocolate?'

For a moment her face looked blank with surprise, and then she smiled. 'Yes, I would. Thank you.'

As we were sipping the creamy-hot drinks, I said, 'Mum? At the hearing, did you talk to Dad, at all?'

Mum blew on her chocolate, took a small sip. 'Very briefly.'

I didn't know what to ask. How is he? Did he mention me? Does he hate me now? I swallowed. 'Well . . . what did he say?'

She looked down at her cup, swirled the chocolate around. 'He's still very hurt.'

That Saturday, I didn't have play practice for a change, because the understudies were having a rehearsal. I lay on the settee, bored, playing Minesweeper on my mobile.

The mobile's brand new. A snazzy pink one with electric-blue flowers on it. Mum unplugged our phone days ago – it was always reporters, begging and pleading for us to talk to them. When I pointed out that this was all right for *Mum* because she had a mobile, but it made it a tad hard for *me* to have a social life, she bought me a mobile of my own.

Dad had always said I couldn't have one, that he didn't care if I was the only teenager in the universe who didn't.

So that was one good thing, anyway. Except the

buttons were too little and fiddly to really play properly.

I tossed the phone to one side, rolled over and glared at the ceiling. I had done all my homework. There was a SATS study sheet I could do for science, but I couldn't be bothered. I was *bored*.

Without moving, I fumbled for the remote and switched the TV on. Two boring-looking men in suits, droning away. I was just about to change the channel when I heard one of them say, ' . . . the present explosive case of Child X.'

No! Not *again!* I just wanted to watch *The Simpsons* or something!

'Mmm, yes,' said the other. 'If a man finds out that he is not the father of a child he believed to be his—'

I lunged for the remote and switched them off. Yes, I *know* Dad isn't my dad, I'm never allowed to forget it! I clutched a blue cushion over my face and let out a padded shriek. I was sick of thinking about it all the time, sick of being cooped up in the house, having to have Gran with me everywhere I went! Dad, how could you *do* this to me? You've ruined my life!

A delicious, forbidden idea popped into my mind. I dropped the cushion and sat up, heart racing. Gran was asleep. And Mum was out shopping.

I went into the kitchen and peeked out the back window. I didn't see any photographers, but they had sussed out our trick with the garden wall early on, so you had to be careful going out that way. I was already putting on my coat and scarf as I thought this; strapping my handbag on to my shoulders. *Out*, I was going *out!*

I scribbled a quick note:

Dear Mum and Gran,
DON'T worry, I'm OK! I've just gone for a walk
because I'm totally sick of being stuck in the house.
I promise to avoid the photographers! See you soon.
Jules.

I slipped out the back door, locking it behind me with my key, and eased through the garden, listening. The grass was longer without Dad here. It muffled my steps. I kept my eyes on the wall, scanning it for roaming flash bulbs waiting to go off. Suddenly I was Agent JC, on the case.

I got to the bottom of the garden and peered over the wall, eyes narrowed. *Agent JC scanned the scene with eagle eyes. No-one there. Still, a little backup wouldn't hurt . . . and she slowly drew her .45 from her trenchcoat pocket. Cocked it.*

'Right,' I muttered. 'Come on, guys . . . make my day.'

I braced my hands on the wall and jumped, rolling over it and dropping to the other side in one smooth motion. Or at least that was the plan. *Ouch.* I rubbed my leg. It looks so easy doing it that way in the films!

Halfway through the neighbour's garden, I saw a camera pointing at me from the side of their house. 'Child X, here!' called the photographer.

Caught! I ducked back behind their house and started to run up the other side, then realized that of course there *wasn't* another side; it was semi-detached like ours. So I flung myself at their side garden wall to get into *their* neighbour's yard, but it was too high for me, and the photographer was right behind me, snapping away.

You'll never take me alive, growled Agent JC!

I turned and charged him with my head down, barrelling into his soft stomach.

'Oof!' He staggered backwards, stumbling over his feet. His camera landed on the ground with a sharp *crack.* Excellent! I cut back, scooped it up and dodged past him, back up the side yard and then burst out into the street, with him swearing and shouting behind me.

'Come back with that! That's an expensive camera, that is!'

I was laughing so hard I could hardly run, but it still wasn't any great trick outrunning *him.* He must have weighed about fifteen stone. He started groaning and gasping before we even got to the end of the road. I turned around and skipped backwards, snapping his picture. *Whirr, whirr.*

'Smile!' I called.

He bellowed, propelling himself forward with a hefty lurch. I legged it onto Latman Avenue, then plunged into an alley and came out onto Chapman Street, doubling back and forth until I got to the high street. When I finally looked around, my heavy panting shadow had disappeared.

Victory!

Chapter Sixteen

As I passed the bus stop on the high street (still half-jogging in case Fat Bloke somehow managed to catch me up), a bus squealed to this perfect James Bond halt beside me, flinging its doors open. I dived onto it, and bounded upstairs to look out of the back window. Yup, there he was – Fat Bloke, just rounding the corner. I banged really hard on the window and waved at him as we pulled away, but I don't think he saw me.

I flopped down into a seat, ignoring the two old ladies with their shopping who sat scowling at me, and wondered where I was going. Somewhere *interesting*, hopefully. I played with the camera, taking snaps of passing shops. And then about half an hour later, I started to see familiar streets. Uncle Derek lived near here.

I jumped up and yanked the cord. I hadn't seen Uncle Derek for *ages*, and suddenly he was exactly the person I wanted to see. I clambered down the metal staircase, and hopped off the bus as it came to a stop. I wanted to tell him all about the play. He was the only one who would *totally* understand what it meant to me. And I wanted to hear about his series, and tease him about that stupid beard he had to grow. I wanted to be Lady Horseface and Sir Twaddle for a bit, and not even *mention* the letter 'X'.

Having craftily lost her arch-enemy, The Fat Bloke, Agent JC slipped furtively up the steps to the terraced house and pressed against the doorway. She scanned the street up and down, her eyes mere slits, and swiftly took vital surveillance photos.

Whirr, whirr. Picture of the bin. Picture of my hand. Oh, good stuff, sir! Thank you, thank you. I bowed to an invisible audience, sweeping the camera up into the air behind me. I bounced up again, giggling like a loon, and rang the bell. Not forgetting the secret agent password buzz, of course.

DINGdongDINGdongdingdingding.

'All right, I'm *coming!*' shouted a voice.

I grinned as I heard Uncle Derek stomping towards the door. When the door to his terraced house flew open, I was ready for him, camera poised.

SNAP! 'Smile, Sir Twaddle!'

'*Awk!*' He slammed the door shut. 'Go away! I'm not speaking to the press!'

I stood there holding the camera, staring at the smooth wood of the closed door. I could hear him breathing.

I knocked. 'Uncle Derek? It's me, Jules. I was just messing about.'

The door opened a cautious crack. A blue eye

peered out at me. 'You're alone?'

No, wait – the game's over now; we're not playing secret agents anymore.

'Yes, it's just me.'

He eased the door open a tiny bit more and stood staring down at me like an affronted Viking, with his bristling red beard. 'What did you think you were *doing?*'

I held up the camera. 'Look, a war trophy. I got it off this photographer who was chasing me—'

His freckles jumped out against his skin. He hustled me inside, banging the door shut behind us. 'My God, you didn't bring the *press* here, did you?' He peeked out the little window on his door.

'No, I told you – I lost him ages ago.'

Uncle Derek turned and looked at me with his lips pressed together. He didn't say a word.

Confused, I kept on: 'I was just fed up with staying home all the time, and Gran was asleep, and Mum was out, so I just thought . . .'

'All right, all right.' He ran a large hand through his hair. 'Let's go and sit down.'

But when we went into the lounge, he saw my handbag hanging from my shoulders. And became very weird.

'What's *that?*' he snapped.

'What?' I turned and looked behind me. Nothing; just a sleek wide-screen TV and a leather armchair.

'*That!*' He motioned with his hand.

And before I could answer, he went absolutely mental, pacing about the hardwood floor with his voice echoing around the room: 'Juliet, you *cannot* move in here. My God, can you imagine the negative press – I'm just on the verge of my big break! I can't have it. It's impossible. And the responsibility, there's that too. No, I can't do it; I *won't*. I'm never at home, it wouldn't work, it—'

'Uncle Derek! It's a *handbag*!'

He stopped, frowning, and pointed a theatrical finger. '*That* is a *backpack*!'

I put the camera on the floor and pulled off my handbag. I suppose it looks a *bit* like a backpack, but honestly! I opened it over the black leather sofa, shaking it. My wallet and hairbrush fell out. A little photo album that Marty had given me. A Snickers bar.

'There, all right? I don't want to move in with you! I just, like, *happened* to come here! No big deal.'

Slowly, his broad shoulders relaxed. He dropped onto the black leather sofa and let out a long, puttery breath. 'Right. Well – sit down and tell me what happened.'

So I did. All about the photographers, and the great escape from Fat Bloke. I even jumped up and acted bits out for him, being Agent JC on the case. I thought he's find it *amusing* or something. But he just sat there rubbing his jaw, smiling tensely. Like he was waiting for me to spring the bad news on him. What was *wrong* with him, anyway?

'So, well, that's what happened,' I finished lamely, flopping back on to the sofa. My hairbrush and stuff bounced. I wondered if he was ever going to offer me something to drink. Or eat. I was starving.

Uncle Derek looked away. 'Yes, it's all been a bit terrible with the press, hasn't it? I've been seeing it in the papers, on TV . . . I've, ah – been meaning to ring, actually. But I've been busy with the last episode of the series. And with publicity.'

He nodded at a copy of *Entertainment Magazine* that lay on his chrome and glass coffee table. He was on the front cover, big and smiling, with his arm around the toothy blonde actress who plays his wife.

'Wow.' I picked it up and flipped through it.

He cleared his throat. 'Page thirty-one.'

And there it was, a whole article about him: **In The Ascendant and Rising Fast.** *Derek Cheney has been a professional actor for years, with numerous TV, film and stage roles under his belt – so why are we only now hearing about this amazingly talented actor?*

'Wow,' I said again. 'That's great. You must be really chuffed.'

'Yes.' Uncle Derek took the magazine from me and looked down at the article, turning the page and scanning the lines as though he had never seen them before.

'So – well, Jules, look. *You're* an actress, you'll understand. I can't have the negative publicity of – of being associated with all of this. Do you see? It could ruin everything I've worked towards for over a decade now.' He put the magazine down, arranging it to a careful right angle with the table edge.

I stared at him. 'You . . . want me to leave, don't you?'

He jumped up and rubbed his hands against his baggy khaki trousers, looking over at the vacant screen of the TV set. 'Well, actually, I think it might be best. I mean, from what you say, that photographer bloke is probably still trying to find you. Not to mention the rest of them, if they've heard about what's happened. You understand, don't you?'

A heavy weight tightened in my throat. 'Um – yeah. I understand.' I shoved everything back in my bag and picked up the camera again. Even though it seemed like a stupid thing to be carrying around now, somehow.

He walked me to the door. His blue eyes flickered on me, and then away. 'I was – happy with things the way they were, you know. And perhaps maybe, someday—' he stopped, and shook his head. 'But not now. I'm sorry. Not now.'

So much for Sir Twaddle and Lady Horseface. He didn't even drive me to the bus stop.

I wasn't secret agent JC anymore. I was just Jules, and the heater on the bus was broken, and the trip took ages. I pressed my face against the steamed-up window, telling myself that I shouldn't feel so hurt. His career was just taking off. Yes, but he has a *niece* as well as a career, doesn't he? Or OK, maybe I wasn't really his niece, but didn't he care about me at all?

I wiped my eyes. You can tell he's Dad's brother, all right – they both ditched me at the first sign of trouble. Like rats scurrying off a sinking ship. I was *delighted* not to be related to the pair of them. Who'd want to be?

I was walking home from the bus stop when Mum's car pulled up. 'Jules! I've been looking everywhere for you!'

Ah. Oh dear. I got in the car, rehearsing excuses in my head. See, I got really fed up with these men in suits on TV, so I was being a secret agent, and . . .

Mum's face was pale, with her dark hair stark against it. She put the car in gear and looked over her shoulder, pulling out into the traffic. 'Where have you *been*? We've had a photographer from the *Clarion* banging on the front door, shouting that you stole his camera—'

Her eyes went to my lap. The camera perched neatly on my knees like a polite lapdog.

She looked at me. 'Jules, you—'

'I was being a secret agent,' I said weakly.

She didn't say anything for a moment. Then her shoulders started to shake. She pulled the car into a lay-by and bent over the steering wheel, hiding her face in her arms. Her shoulders heaved.

'Mum?'

Muffled cries choked from her throat. Terrified, I touched her arm. 'Mum, don't cry, it's OK—'

'Oh!' she raised her head. And she wasn't crying, she was in absolute hysterics! 'Oh Jules – the look on his face – he said you – you took his photo!' She whooped again and fell back in her seat, snorting and gasping. I watched in amazement. I hadn't seen Mum laugh like that since before Dad left. *Long* before. Years, maybe.

Finally she sat up and wiped her eyes. 'We'll have to give him his camera back, of course.'

I was laughing too by then. 'No, it's mine! It's a spoil of war.'

She took it from me, clicked open a compartment at the back and pulled out a black snake-strip of film. She dangled it in front of me and smiled. 'No. *This* is.'

Lunchtimes were lonely. I sat in the library by myself, eating cold ham sandwiches from home. Because when I told Marty that Mrs Greaves had said she could eat in there with me, her face went all surprised and stricken.

'But—' she stopped and tried to smile. 'Um . . . yeah, great,' she said feebly.

Of course it turned out that The Weedy One had asked Marty to eat lunch with *him*. And even though she said, 'Don't be silly, you're my best friend, I'd *far* rather be with you,' I could tell she was gutted.

We were walking to the library by then. I stopped, and pointed her back towards the canteen. 'Look, go ahead. I'll be fine. Really.'

Her face flowered into a smile. '*Really?* You don't mind? Are you sure?'

So that was the routine we'd settled into for almost two weeks now – she'd say 'Are you *sure* you don't mind? I feel like such a louse!' And I'd say yes, I'm sure, and end up eating alone again, hiding from the photographers all by myself.

Cow.

I sighed and flipped through a *Teen* magazine, munching my dreary sandwich. Behind me, I heard some kids come in, and Mr Patel tell them to leave.

'But why aren't we allowed in? *Jules* is allowed in.'

Vicki! My muscles tightened. I looked over my shoulder, and met her smirky blue eyes. She looked right at me as she said, 'There's a programme on BBC1 we want to see in the media centre. A *really* interesting one.'

'Well, I'm afraid you're going to miss it.' Mr Patel started herding them out.

Two guesses what the programme had to be about. I felt sick, but I gritted my teeth and gave Vicki a look of total disdain. Like, you utter saddoid, trying to keep getting at me all the time.

'I'll get my mum to record it, shall I?' said Anne as they left.

'Ooh, yes. Can't miss the latest on X.'

Mr Patel shut the door and stood there for a moment, rubbing his bald head. 'I'm sorry that – that you're going through this, Juliet. I'll have a word with Mrs Greaves about Vicki.'

'Don't bother.' I looked down at my sandwich. I couldn't eat another bite, I'd be ill. I scraped back my chair and stood up. 'Could I see what's on TV?'

His head whipped up. 'What? I really don't think—'

'It's about me, isn't it?'

The media centre was at the far end of the library, a glass-partitioned room with a couple of cassette decks. A TV and VCR. Mr Patel unlocked the door and motioned to the chairs. 'Do you want me to stay with you?'

I shook my head. He started to say something else, but didn't. The door clicked behind him as he left. I sat down on the hard wooden chair and pressed a button on the remote.

The show was *Yolanda Hayes*, one of those unbearably American-type chat shows, where everyone sits about baring their souls for the nation. And guess what the subject was today?

They spent the first quarter hour discussing the case, talking to expert solicitors and psychiatrists and that sort of thing, who all agreed it was just horrible, horrible. Yolanda grimaced at the camera a lot, tutting and shaking her bright blonde head. She kept saying, 'But it's the *child* we must consider!'

The child squirmed in her seat. Please *don't* consider me, please just go away!

Twelve twenty-seven. I only had three more minutes of lunch. I was reaching for the remote when Yolanda turned to the cameras and said, 'And now, we have a special guest who can perhaps throw some insight on the central question in this tragic case: *Who is Child X's real father?*'

I froze with my hand still in the air. As the audience applauded, my hand slowly moved back into my lap, where it twisted at my burgundy school blazer.

A smiling brown-haired woman came onstage and sat down, crossing her legs. Yolanda introduced her as Nancy – '*Not* her real name,' she cautioned solemnly. 'But Nancy knew the couple who are now

Mr and Mrs X at university, didn't you, Nancy?'

The woman nodded. 'Yes, I did. I was – um – Mrs X's roommate at the time, so I knew them quite well. It was always sort of a rocky relationship; I was amazed when they actually got married.'

'So you were friends with them both?'

'Yes, with the three of them.'

'*Three* of them?' wondered Yolanda in a syrupy voice.

'Yes, with Mr and Mrs X . . . and Mr X's brother.'

A scandalized gasp flew through the studio audience. Yolanda turned to the camera, wide-eyed. 'You don't mean . . .?'

Nancy's chin bobbed eagerly. She leaned forward a bit. 'Yes, I think so. I mean, I don't have any proof, but I know that the X's had a huge row just before the wedding, and that Mrs X went out with Derek – oh, sorry. With Mr X's brother. They came back late that night and they had been drinking – and he was still there the next morning. Hol— Mrs X was terribly upset after that. She cried all day, and kept saying what a horrible mistake she had made. But she made me promise not to tell, and married Mr X just a week later.'

A stitch on my blazer hem ripped as I pulled at it. It's not true. It's not true. Not Mum and Uncle Derek, please no . . .

Yolanda said, 'And as it turns out, Mr X's brother – let's call him Mr Y, shall we? Mr Y is quite a well-known television star, isn't he, Nancy? What do you think when you see him on TV?'

Mr Patel cleared his throat. I jumped. I hadn't even heard him open the door. He reached past me and turned off the TV, and then his arms hung helplessly. 'Juliet – Jules—'

I sprang up. 'I have to get to class. Thanks for – for letting me watch.'

We were making soup in Domestic Science. It's a huge classroom, with dozens of hobs and work counters. Everyone was rustling about with their ingredients, getting knives and chopping boards ready.

I slowly unpacked my Sainsbury's bag. Uncle Derek. Mum and Uncle Derek. It wasn't true, it couldn't be true.

'What did you bring?' whispered Marty. She had just taken a head of broccoli and some cheese out of her bag.

I had to look at it to remember. 'Ham and leek.'

Mrs Vines clapped her hands. 'Less talking, please! Now, before you start chopping your ingredients, let's just go over the game plan, shall we?'

She started talking about what makes good soup, and how you knew whether to use a milk or broth base, and how to thicken it if you needed to. Her words blurred together senselessly. Mum, going out with Uncle Derek before her wedding . . .

Then, slowly at first, I noticed people glancing out the window. And then at me. Vicki turned and smiled at me. Fear hit me like an anvil. What *now?* What else could possibly be happening?

'What's going on?' I muttered to Marty. We were at

the back of the room, over to one side, and I couldn't see over people's heads.

Marty waited until Mrs Vines turned to write something on the whiteboard, and then stretched up on her tiptoes, peering to see. 'I think . . .' She dropped back down and stared at me. 'Jules, there's a *news crew* out there with the photographers!'

I stood statue-still. A news crew.

It had just got worse. It had actually got *worse*. Uncle Derek, and now a news crew. No. Stop. Please make it stop!

'. . . Jules?' whispered Marty.

I didn't answer. I very calmly took off my apron and put it on the counter.

Marty's voice became tinged with alarm. 'Jules, are you OK?' she hissed.

No. I'm not OK. I've had enough. Up at the front, Mrs Vines was still talking about how to make tasty soup, drawing green bullet-points on the board and nodding at something Janet was saying. She wasn't looking my way but I don't think I would have cared if she had been.

Leaving Marty gaping like a fish behind me, I picked up my bag and left.

Chapter Seventeen

No-one came after me. I was the only person in the world, walking through the silent corridors. I shouldered my bag and kept walking, down the stairs and then outside into the early spring sun. I didn't plan it at all; my feet just automatically took me around the back of the science building and then over to the car park by the main entrance. I walked in the grass alongside the low fence, half-hidden by trees and cars.

I could see them all there on the other side of the fence – nine or ten bored-looking photographers hanging about at their usual stations, ready to catch me after the last bell. And a TV camera, bristling on its owner's shoulder like a weird space creature. Coils of black cable snaked all over tarmac.

A dark-skinned woman with sleek black hair and a yellow suit stood in front of the photographers, facing the TV camera with her back half to me. No-one had seen me yet. As I got closer, I could hear her saying in a posh TV voice:

'This is Sheena Khan. Behind me is the scene at a secondary school somewhere in southern England,

where a teenager caught in one of the most controversial court cases of the decade continues to be
hounded by the tabloid press—'

'That's her!' cried someone.

Heads swivelled towards me. The photographers
grabbed for their cameras, pointing and snapping,
setting off flash bulbs. Sheena Khan stopped mid-
sentence and turned around, looking at me with her
perfect black eyebrows raised.

I climbed over the fence and walked through the
crowd of photographers. They bubbled about me like
boiling water, snapping away. The TV camera
swivelled towards me.

I walked up to Sheena Khan. She wasn't much taller
than I was.

'Um, hi. I'm Child X. Only my real name is Juliet
Cheney. And I want to say something.'

Scurry, action! 'Keep filming,' barked Sheena. 'Some-
body get a mike on her!' A blue-jeaned assistant leapt at
me, clipped a tiny microphone to my blazer. Someone
else started to powder my nose. Sheena brushed them
away.

'Don't bother with that; we'll have to black her face
out anyway. Right, hon.' Sheena put her arm around
me. 'Look at the camera and have your say.'

The camera waited, like a dark tunnel pointed at
me. I straightened my shoulders and the words were
there, waiting for me:

'I want everyone to leave me alone. And to leave
my family alone. It's horrible enough anyway, finding out that my dad isn't my dad, and that – that

maybe my uncle is, and that Dad is suing Mum – but all of this is just making it a million times worse. I mean, I know it's a big court case, so you probably have to report on it, but you don't need pictures of my *house*, and – and, please just *leave us alone!*'

Sheena paused a beat, and then gazed at the camera and said, 'An impassioned plea, Child X. Can you tell me if—'

'My name's *Jules*,' I clenched out. Flashbulbs were going off all around us as we spoke.

Sheena's manicured nails dug into my arm. She smiled at the camera. 'Of course, I'm sorry. Jules, can you tell me who it is you're speaking to? The British public, or the press?'

'I don't know. Both. I just want everyone to stop *talking* about me.'

She nodded, dark eyes swimming with sympathy. (Ha!) 'Jules, you mentioned your uncle just now. Do you mean that—'

'Stop this *instantly!*' bellowed a voice.

We turned and saw Mrs Greaves running across the car park towards us. The photographers whirled to face her. *Snapsnapsnap!!* One of them fumbled to reload his camera. 'Keep running, you lovely old dear,' he muttered under his breath.

'Keep filming,' ordered Sheena at the TV camera.

The cameraman chuckled. 'As if I'd *stop!*'

Mrs Greaves got to the fence and fought her way over it with all the cameras pointed at her, clicking and whirring. She was nowhere near as nimble as she had been with our back garden wall. Finally she made it over and strode up to us, flushing dark red, with her hair wisping about her face.

'This is illegal. I demand that you stop this instantly and destroy the film. Juliet, come back to class now.'

Sheena glinted at her. 'And you are . . .?'

Mrs Greaves kept her gaze rigidly away from the TV camera. 'Sandra Greaves, the headmistress of Juliet's school. Juliet, come with me. Your mother is going to be *extremely* upset.'

She took my arm, pulling at me. Sheena's hand tightened around my shoulder.

'Shouldn't Jules have something to say about that?'

'No, she shouldn't!'

'Jules, can you comment on whether—'

Suddenly I heard myself screaming. 'Leave me alone! Everybody! Just leave me alone!'

I broke away from them both, twisting out of Sheena's grasp. The microphone popped off my lapel. I stumbled a step as Mrs Greaves made a grab for me, but then I was away, running, my feet churning against the pavement. Down the street, past the shops, shoving past pedestrians. My bag thudded against my side.

'Catch her!' cried someone.

Without stopping, I looked over my shoulder. They were all running after me, the news crew and Mrs Greaves and *everyone*. I ran faster, streaking down the pavement. I could hear them all behind me, shouting at each other. It was like something in a nightmare. Or the Keystone Kops.

I sped around a corner and skidded as I stopped running, walking quickly and trying to blend into the crowd. Yes, with your phone-box red *hair*! I lunged into a bookshop, heart hammering as I strolled back towards the paperbacks.

I picked one up and opened it, holding it over my face as I peeked around its side.

The photographers were standing across the street. One of them was looking towards the top of the high street; another one shook his head and pointed over at the bookshop. As I watched, Mrs Greaves panted up, and then a moment later Sheena Khan appeared, tottering on her high heels. They all started across the street towards the shop.

No! I put the book back on the shelf and moved further back into the shop, looking around wildly. STAFF ONLY, said a door against the back wall. I slipped into it, closing the door behind me.

A chubby girl about sixteen or so sat on a table smoking a cigarette. She stared at me. 'You're not supposed to be in here.'

I forced a giggle. The room was sloping and dingy, filled with untidy piles of paperbacks. 'I'm hiding from my friend. Is there a back door or something?' Outside the door, I could hear the murmur of questions. I pictured them streaming up the aisles, cameras cocked, ready to film the capture of Child X.

The girl chuckled. SHERRY, read her plastic name-tag. 'What, have you done a runner from school or something?' She motioned to a grey door behind her.

'That's the service door. Hit the button first or the alarm will go off.'

'Thank you!' I gasped, and leapt for it. Just as I smacked the button and dived out, I heard a volley of knocks erupt on the staff door behind me. Too late! I was away, racing up the street. I ducked into an alley and peered back, panting, watching the nondescript door I had just come out of.

No-one.

I was free.

I walked for hours after that, not thinking about where I was going. After a while I didn't even know. Finally, I came to an empty playground, and sat down on one of the swings, twirling it back and forth. Streetlights were starting to come on.

Hot, grainy sand filled my throat. Mum and Uncle Derek. Uncle Derek, my father. No wonder he freaked out when I turned up on his doorstep! He thought I was about to start calling him *Dad*.

Suddenly it seemed completely obvious, like everyone except me had always known. (Yes, she does resemble her father quite strongly, doesn't she? Her *real* father, not that bloke she calls Dad, poor misguided child.')

And Mum . . . I probed carefully at the thought, like a bruise. Mum and Uncle Derek. A terrible mistake; she had cried all day.

I twirled back and forth for what seemed like ages, letting the chains twine above me. I didn't know what to think, or feel. Except . . . Mum wasn't the one hurting me now. Mum wasn't the one who had turned me into Child X.

If I knew where Dad was, I'd . . . I twisted the swing hard, shoving at the ground with my foot. I wanted to hurt him. Really *hurt* him, so that his insides felt ragged and empty, and he knew how I had been feeling for months now. And then I'd laugh. I'd say: see? Not very nice, is it?

I should have told Sheena Khan that. I should have let Dad hear it on the news, how *glad* I was that he had gone.

I shivered, huddling into my thin blazer, and noticed for the first time how dark it had got. Where was I, anyway? I stood up and started walking again, looking for a bus stop. When I finally found one, the next bus wasn't for almost an hour, and I wasn't even sure it was the right one.

It was after eight o'clock by then, and inky dark. Fear prickled at my neck. I stood under the amber streetlight rubbing my arms, and every few seconds a car zoomed past, washing me in horrible-smelling fumes.

A drunken businessman lurched up to me. 'You all alone, pet?'

I looked away, trembling with the cold and something else.

'Eee, you could be friendlier than that, couldn't you? Eh?'

Go away, please, please . . . I didn't say anything and finally he went, muttering to himself about the sullen south.

I hugged myself. I'm so scared. I'm so scared. And then in a sudden flash of brain-lightning, I remembered my new mobile phone. I scrambled to find it in my bag and switched it on, beep beep! – and there were *four* text messages for me, three from Mum and one from Marty.

The one from Marty said, J, U WERE ON THE NEWS! R U OK? EVRY1 IS LOOKING 4 U!

On the news . . . my stomach iced over. Now I'd have a news crew at home, too, tracking my every move. *Child X, live and in colour.* What had I *done?* Finally I checked Mum's messages. All three of them were pretty much the same, asking me to please please ring her and let her know I was all right.

She answered before the first ring had finished. 'Hello?'

I clutched the phone. 'Mum, it's me! I'm lost, can you please come get me?' And then I started to cry.

Mum made me walk around a bit, reading out street signs to her until she could suss out from the A-Z where I was. Then she told me to keep talking to her until I found a nice-looking restaurant, and to go in and order a coffee or something until she got there. But to stay on the phone with her until I did, to make sure the waitress would serve me.

'Be careful, keep in the street lights,' she kept saying. I could practically *hear* her chain-smoking down the line until I told her I was in a nice, bright coffee bar.

'Right. Now, just sit tight, and I'll be there as soon as I can.'

So I had a cappuccino, which I've never had before, and Mum got there about forty-five minutes later. Her eyes looked puffy and sore. She slid into the booth beside me and hugged me hard. She smelled like perfume, cold cashmere, cigarette smoke. Mum-smells.

I closed my eyes tightly, holding back tears. 'Mum, I didn't mean to run away again, I promise.'

'I know, sweetie . . . I know.'

I didn't have to tell her what had happened. She had already heard from Mrs Greaves. Not to mention seeing it for herself, she said, pretty much non-stop on the news all day.

I told her about Yolanda Hayes, though. The words crept out haltingly: 'This woman, they called her Nancy, came on. She, um . . . said she was your roommate at university. And that she knew you and Dad. And Uncle Derek.'

I looked at her. Her eyes were brimming. 'It's true, I'm afraid. Oh, Jules, I'm sorry – what a horrible way to find out.'

I nodded. No arguments there.

She wiped her eyes. 'I'm glad you know, though,' she said quietly. 'I wanted to tell you when you first found out about all this. But Derek rang me up when Ben left – that's when we had lunch together that time – and literally begged me not to tell you, to keep it all totally quiet. He said he couldn't deal with fatherhood, and that it would ruin his career if it came out. And . . . I felt so torn. You had a right to know the truth, but I thought maybe *he* had rights that should be respected, too. Oh, I don't know.' She rubbed her forehead with tense, white fingers.

I picked up the saltcellar, skating it about the table in little circles. 'I just can't get my head around it. I mean – you and Uncle *Derek*.'

She gave a snorting sort of laugh, and pushed her fringe back. 'Oh, Jules, me neither! Someday maybe you'll understand, things can happen that you *never* would have imagined yourself doing, that you're just so appalled by afterwards—'

I wiped a grain of salt from the rim, rubbed it between my fingers. 'No, I – I think maybe I understand now, sort of.'

Her eyes – brown with green glints, so much like mine – cut across to me. 'Then you don't hate me?'

I leaned against her. I was so tired. Maybe I *should* have hated her – cheating on Dad with his own brother. But Mum was just Mum. She was trying. OK, she made a mistake thirteen and a bit years ago; deal with it.

I shook my head. 'No, I don't hate you.'

Mum let out a shaky breath. 'Thank you, sweetie,' she whispered.

She let me have a lovely long lie-in the next morning. I didn't wake up until around ten o'clock. I lay in bed, cuddled in my duvet, and felt almost normal again.

Mum was sitting at the dining table when I went downstairs, with her eyes far away and her lips pressed against her index fingers. An almost-full cup of coffee. with the milk skimmed over on top sat in front of her.

She roused herself when she saw me, and smiled. 'Morning. How did you sleep?'

'Like a log.' I helped myself to a satsuma from the crystal bowl and sat down across from her, peeling it. The lovely sweet-sharp orange smell leapt out. I looked around. 'Where's Gran?'

'Upstairs packing.'

'What for?'

Mum glanced down at her cold coffee, sighed and pushed it away. 'Because we're probably not going to need her here for much longer, and she wants to get back to her own house. Jules . . . Ben rang last night, after you went to bed. And then again about half an hour ago.'

I stopped peeling and looked at her.

'He saw you on TV, and wanted to make sure you were all right. He's decided to drop the court case.'

At first I could hardly take it in. And then a hurricane of relief roared through me, sweeping me up and carrying me away on its crest. Dad had dropped the case! *I wasn't Child X anymore!* It was over, it was really *over*.

'And he wants to see you.'

My elation evaporated.

'. . . Oh.' I turned the satsuma over in my hands, poking at the orange cushions of fruit with a finger.

'Do you want to see him?'

My feelings twisted around in a jumble. Dad

chopping onions and pausing to point his knife at me, looking stern but laughing underneath. And then leaning stiff and angry against his motorcycle, not caring in the least that I was Lyra.

Turning me into Child X.

'Do you?' pressed Mum gently.

I shrugged.

Neither of us said anything for a moment. Finally she touched my hand. 'I think you should, but I'm not going to force you. I'll tell him that you need time to think about it, all right?'

I slowly pulled away a satsuma section. Little orange drops popped up from a tear in its fabric.

'Jules? Is it all right if I tell him that? Or do you want me to tell him something else? Or *you* could talk to him, if—'

I shook my head. 'No. Just tell him that.'

Chapter Eighteen

CHILD X MEDIA SHAME

 ' . . . I didn't realize she had gone,' said the Domestic Science teacher whose class Child X left without permission. 'It's quite a large class, and I had already taken the register. Then another girl suddenly called out that she could see Child X through the window, heading towards the cameras, so of course I immediately went for the headmistress . . .'

'PLEASE LEAVE US ALONE,' PLEADS CHILD X
Court Case Dropped After Surprise Television Appeal

BBC2: *Newsnight:* **'In the Wake of Child X'** Is DNA testing fair to children? Neil Baines explores new issues thrown up by a very old question: is this really my child?

'. . . the teenager is now home safe and sound, but following her emotional breakdown on national TV yesterday, we are left with some disturbing questions regarding our own appetite for outrage . . .'

*

'Jules . . . come here and look at this,' called Mum.

I still hadn't got dressed; we were having a lazy day. Well, lazy – I was doing a SATS study sheet at the dining table. Maths comprehension, fascinating stuff. I looked up, not really paying attention, just in time to see her sweep the curtains open in the front room. Sunlight streamed in for the first time in weeks.

'Mum, what are you *doing!*' Photographers peering in, taking pictures of me in my ratty old yellow dressing-gown! I scrambled over to pull the curtains closed, reached past Mum's arm. And stopped. I stood beside Mum and saw . . . our front garden.

The photographers had gone.

'No, wait – there's one,' said Mum, pointing. Sure enough, a bored-looking man with a beard stood near our car, holding a camera.

'One,' I breathed out. We looked at each other.

'One!' screeched Mum. 'We only have *one photographer* in front of our house!' And it was completely silly and childish, but we grabbed each other and started dancing and jumping about, laughing, both of us still in our dressing-gowns.

That Saturday, we had a full dress rehearsal at the Flying Frog, which means that we were in costume, plus they were testing out all the lights and special effects and stuff. They had some *incredibly* cool ones – like a screen behind us that showed slides of spinning dials when Lyra consulted her truth-compass, and pictures of wildcats and moths as Adrian mimed changing form.

'It's looking very, very good,' said Diane, after we finished the first run-through. 'You can all be really proud of yourselves. You're in top form for opening night on Friday week.' We all rolled our eyes and grimaced at each other as we sat around on the stage.

'*But . . .?*' intoned Adrian from across the circle, giving the word about three syllables.

Diane grinned and consulted her clipboard. '*But . . .* I do have just a few *really minor* points, all right? Mike, on your first entrance, could you—'

Suddenly, a wedge of sunlight streamed across the semi-darkened audience, then fell away again with the muffled clank of a door closing. Diane frowned and hopped down from the stage, leaving her clipboard behind. 'Hello, who's there?'

'Quick, grab her clipboard,' said Mike. 'Obliterate all of her horrible little notes.'

Lesley, who was closer to it, leaned *way* over, raising blonde eyebrows as she looked at Diane's scribbles. 'Oh, dearie me . . . yes, you should be *very* worried, Mike . . .'

'Oi!' Mike scrambled up. 'What does she say?'

I was laughing with the others when Diane's voice pierced through: 'No, absolutely not. I'm afraid I have to ask you to leave.'

Mike stopped in his steps, looking over the side. Instant silence fell across the stage as we all pricked our ears.

A man's voice: 'Yes, I know, and I do understand – but if I could just see her for a moment—'

Dad.

Everything around me dissolved. I stood up without realizing what I was doing. Went to the edge of the stage and hopped down.

He and Diane were standing in the entrance of the fire door. When Dad saw me, he stopped talking. His throat moved as he swallowed. Diane turned around. Her freckles were arranged in an unfamiliar, worried pattern.

I walked slowly over to them. Dad looked just the same. Well, he would do, wouldn't he? He left in January, and it was only March now. But even so, it was weird to see him looking so unchanged. Rumpled, curly brown hair. Jeans. A faded green T-shirt, his battered leather jacket.

Dad.

Diane said, 'Jules, I'm not at all happy about this; I don't have your mother's permission for you to see him here—'

'No, it's OK,' I said faintly. 'She wouldn't mind. She thinks I should talk to him; she said so.'

Diane's mouth pursed in an anxious frown as she looked at Dad and then back at me. 'All right,' she decided finally, not sounding even remotely convinced. 'But you have to talk here in the theatre, Mr Cheney; I can't have you taking her anywhere.'

Dad's gaze tore away from me. He nodded. 'Yes, yes, that's fine.'

Diane motioned towards the back of the building. 'Why don't you talk in the last row, where you'll have some privacy? I'll give you your notes later, Jules.

We'll be starting the next run-through in about half an hour.'

She stepped aside to let Dad into the theatre, reaching behind him to shut the fire door, and then left us alone. I heard her jump back onto the stage.

'Right, sorry about that. Where was I?'

'Mike!' chorused a dozen voices.

Dad's hands crept slowly into his jacket pockets, squeaking against the leather. I saw them make fists. His green eyes never left mine. 'Jules—'

And I knew I was going to cry. 'Oh, Dad—' I flung myself at him. He scooped me up and held me tightly. A racketing breath went through him. His hand gripped my head against his chest, rocking me.

'Jules – my baby, I'm so sorry, please forgive me—'

I shoved away from him, and choked out, 'Dad, how could you do that to me? *How?*'

His eyes were wet. He reached for my face, stopped short of it and dropped his hand. 'Come on. We need to talk.'

We sat in the last row. At the front of the theatre, the cast and crew were sprawled about on the stage, looking small and far away, like watching them on TV. Diane's voice came to us faintly, going on about the lighting in scene one.

Dad touched the hem of my tunic. 'Is this your costume? It looks great. You – you look great.'

I looked at him, and didn't say anything.

He took his jacket off, draping it on the seat in front of him, and then clasped his hands together on his knees. 'Right. Well, I—' He tapped his clenched hands on his knees. 'Jules, I don't know how to tell it so you'll understand.'

Try.

I waited.

His expression became complicated as he stared at the stage. 'Right, here it is. I love Derek, I guess, because he's my brother, but I don't *like* him. I don't respect him.'

He slumped back in his seat and looked down at his knees. 'This sounds so naff, trying to put it into words.' His mouth twisted. 'I don't like him, but I was always jealous of him. We were always – trying to get one up on each other, I guess. And I always seemed to be just a few steps behind.'

Down below, Diane's voice buzzed thinly as she pointed at the tallest point of the set, talking about wearing shoes with a good grip in the ballooning scenes.

Dad looked up. He kept his eyes on the stage as he said, 'I felt second best, all the time I was growing up. I tried as hard as I could, but somehow I was never as good as – as this utter phoney who just smiled his way through life.' He snorted. 'It was a bit of a constant bashing to my self-esteem, I'll put it that way.'

I hugged my arms tightly across my chest and glared down at the tiny Diane. Try having your father ask for his money back. That's a pretty good ego-builder, too.

'When Holly and I got married and had you, I thought – I have a wife now, I have a kid, this is my *own* family. They love me, no-one can take them away from me. And even when things started going pear-shaped with Holly, I still had you. Knowing that you were my daughter was – everything to me.'

Dad looked down. His hands were knotted in his lap, the veins standing out like thick string. 'So when I found out the truth – when Holly finally told me what she and Derek had suspected all along – I just went sort of insane. I felt like the two of them had taken you away from me.'

'So why didn't you sue *Uncle Derek?* Why was it just *Mum* who you—'

He gave me a small, wry smile. 'Oh, believe me, I wanted to sue him, too. My solicitor talked me out of it. He said that Derek probably wasn't legally obliged to pay me anything, and that in any event, it would be impossible to prove that he had known. After all, *I* never guessed. Red hair runs in the family . . .'

He scraped his hands through his hair. 'God, this is the hardest part.' With his fingers still clutching at his head, he said slowly, 'When Holly told me, I had to know the truth. Or thought I did. It seemed important at the time.'

He stopped. Dropped his hands, rubbed his finger against his mouth. 'So, I . . .'

'Took hairs from my hairbrush and sent them off to America to be tested,' I finished snidely.

He shut his eyes and nodded. 'When I found out for certain, it was the worst moment of my life. Jules, when I filed the court case, I was lashing out, as hard as possible.' He glanced at me with worried eyes. 'The money was never the point; I just wanted to hurt her as badly as I could. I didn't mean to hurt *you*. I know I did, though. Inexcusably so.'

Well, yes, maybe I was a *tiny* bit hurt. Now that you mention it. The sapphire necklace, glinting up at me from the rubbish bin before I shut the lid on it. Hot, stupid tears started down my face.

Dad stroked one of them away with his knuckle. 'But, Jules – when I saw you on TV, when I heard the agony in your voice, every paternal instinct in me . . . all I wanted to do was come and rescue you, and make you stop hurting.'

My emotions whirled about like leaves in a storm. All right, fine, stop talking about it! I sniffed, swiped at my nose.

'And I realized what a complete fool I've been. Of *course* I'm your father; I raised you. And sure, you've got some of Derek in you – like your acting – but you've got a lot more of me.'

Hurrah. I started to stand up. 'I've got to get back onstage—'

He caught my hand, held it tightly. 'Jules, I understand. I've made a terrible, horrible mistake, and I know it will take time for you to forgive me, but I'll spend the rest of my life proving myself to you if I have to. I'm your father, and I'll always be there for you, like it or not.'

Fury seethed up, bubbled over. I jerked my hand away. 'I *don't* like it. I hate it! You turned me into Child X! You didn't want me for a daughter, well fine! I don't want you for a father, either!'

*

I managed to hold back the tears until I got backstage. Fortunately the meeting had just broken up, with people sort of hanging about and stretching and talking to each other before we did the second run-through, so that no-one really noticed when I went past without saying anything.

Safe in a dark, shadowy corner behind the costume racks, I pressed against the concrete wall and sobbed. Dad. Dad. The tears wrenched out of me. I hadn't even known it was *possible* to cry so hard.

'Jules?' said a voice.

I put a hand over my eyes and turned away, shoulders heaving. I couldn't talk. Adrian touched my arm. 'Jules, what *is* it?'

'Is he still out there?' I gasped out.

'Who?'

'My *father*, of course! My *father*.' I don't know why I was so annoyed with him. Like he could really be expected to know. 'Go and check, please go and check!'

'All right, OK!' He left quickly, rustling past a purple satin dress. A few moments later he was back. 'There's no-one out in the theatre. He's gone, Jules, it's OK, he's gone.'

I sobbed harder. I don't know which I had wanted. For him to be gone, or not.

Adrian leaned against the wall beside me, almost blurring into the shadows in his Pan costume – dark brown trousers and a brown shirt. His eyes were wide and scared. 'Jules, what is it? Can I help?'

I wiped my eyes. Adrian dug in his too-tight trousers and handed me a tissue.

'Th-thanks.' I blew my nose and mopped my face a bit. I'm sure I looked ravishing. All snotty and streaming. I glanced at Adrian. He still reminded me of a chubby puppy, with his brown hair hanging in his eyes, and the trousers pinching into his round waist. But his dark eyes were like his mum's, soft and kind.

I sniffed and swallowed hard. 'It's – it's just that this is the first time I've seen him since – well, since *everything*. And he apologized about the court case, and said he was still my dad, and—' I shook my head, feeling wet and miserable.

A frown touched Adrian's face. 'Well, that's *good* news, isn't it?'

He didn't understand at all. Why couldn't Marty be here? I shifted against the rough concrete wall. 'No. Because . . . he turned me into Child X, he—'

Adrian nodded. 'I know. But—'

Onstage, Diane clapped her hands and called, 'Right, everyone. Five more minutes, and then let's run through it again, from the top.' Pause. 'Wait, where's Jules?' Her voice sounded pinched and anxious suddenly, like she was afraid Dad had nicked me.

'I saw her, she's backstage somewhere,' called Lesley.

Five minutes! I swiped frantically at my eyes and nose. 'Adrian, I have to wash my face.'

He played with one of the hanging costumes, a flouncy thing with lacy sleeves. As if I hadn't spoken, he said, 'Turning you into Child X, yeah, that was really terrible. But if he's sorry . . . I don't know, shouldn't you give him another chance, maybe?'

'No! Not after what he's done—' A sob burst from my throat and I quickly ducked my head.

'Jules, please don't cry! I'm sorry, I didn't mean to make you cry again.' He took my hand and squeezed it.

Adrian, holding my hand. I didn't know what to say, so I didn't say anything. We stood there in the shadows, not really looking at each other, holding hands until it was time to go onstage. His fingers were warm and firm, and slightly sweaty.

It felt nice.

Chapter Nineteen

Vicki came up to me at school that Monday, as I was waiting for Marty outside the art building. 'Hi.'

I looked at her and waited for the snide comment, like, where's your entourage, Miss Star? Or, Are we feeling X-tra special today? But instead she just stood there, fiddling with the strap of her bag. Georgina and Anne and Janet were nowhere in sight. *That* was weird. She looked naked without them.

'Um,' she said finally, flipping her blonde hair back. 'I saw you on TV the other night.'

I shrugged, and stared across the courtyard.

Vicki took a deep breath. 'And – I just wanted to say that I'm sorry. I know I was really . . . I really didn't understand what you were going through. And I think it was really brave of you to do that.'

I stared at her, my mind spinning about like wheels on ice.

She shifted to her other foot, and crossed her arms across her chest. 'And . . . I'm glad the photographers are gone. I mean, glad for you. And – I'm just really sorry, OK?'

My mouth snapped shut. 'Yes, OK. I mean, thanks.'

She nodded stiffly, and walked away.

Vicki Young! Apologizing!

Dad had started ringing every day, like clockwork.

'I don't want to talk to him,' I told Mum whenever she held the phone out to me.

'Jules, I think you should.'

'I have nothing to say.'

She sighed and shook her head, carrying the phone back into the kitchen and murmuring something to Dad.

And then on Friday, I heard her saying, 'Ben, I am *not* keeping her from you; she doesn't want to talk to you! I agree, counselling's a splendid idea; set something up and we'll go—' Her last word came out in a gasp, because I had jumped into the kitchen and grabbed the phone off her.

'Mum's not keeping me from you! How dare you say that! *I don't want to talk to you!*'

'Jules!' Dad took a deep breath. I could just picture him, running a hand through his hair and pacing about. 'All right, I'm sorry, I shouldn't have said that. I was frustrated.'

'Don't apologize to *me*.' I was shaking, I was so angry.

'OK. You're right. Put Holly on and I'll tell her I'm sorry.'

But when I looked around, I saw that Mum had slipped out of the kitchen. Sneak! Traitor! 'She's gone,' I said sulkily.

'I'll apologize to her next time. All right?'

How had I ended up *talking* to him? I longed to hang up so badly that my fingers itched, but I didn't quite have the nerve. I sat down stiffly on the stool.

'Jules, I know you're angry with me, but there's loads that we have to talk about.'

'Like *what?*'

'Well, like I'm moving back to Jameston, for one thing.'

Was I supposed to cheer? 'What for?'

His voice was patient. 'Because I want joint custody, Jules. And it's easier all around if I live there, in terms of your school.'

'Oh, *great*. I don't recall you asking *me* what I thought about it.'

'No, that's right. You don't get a choice on this, I'm afraid. I'm not just going to go away, Jules.'

I jumped up, quivering with rage. 'I wish you would!'

'Jules, darling, I know you're still angry at me, and you have a *right* to be, but—'

'I hate you!' I screamed. 'Don't you *understand*? I hate you! I'll tell the judge that I don't want anything to do with you, that I wish you'd go away and never come back! Leave me alone!' And I banged the kitchen phone down so hard that a bit of plaster cracked away from the wall.

Mum had rushed back into the kitchen when I started shouting. Now she held me as I began crying again. 'Shhh,' she soothed. 'Shhh, it's all right.'

The phone calls stopped. And I was glad.

*

199

'How's your mum doing?' asked Marty. It was the Tuesday before the play. We were leaning against the wall at break, as usual. Except it felt like the Caribbean after being walled up in the library for weeks. The sun was even out.

'She's OK.' I helped myself to some of Marty's smoky bacon crisps. 'Only she's getting really fed up with her job.'

In the courtyard, David was kicking a football about with some of his also-weedy friends. Stick insects at sport. Marty had been sort of watching them, but now she looked back at me. 'I thought she worked from home now.'

'She still has to go into London sometimes, for meetings and that. And she says that whenever she goes into the office now, conversations *stop*. She might go into consultancy work instead, she says.'

'Don't blame her.'

We munched together in silence for a moment. Marty tipped the bag up and shook what was left of the crisps into her mouth. 'Did you see your Uncle Derek on TV last night?'

I frowned. 'No, his show's on *Thursday* night.'

She crinkled the crisp bag up and pitched it towards the bin. Missed.

'No, he was on some sort of celebrity quiz show or something. He was really funny; the audience went completely mad over him. I almost rang you, but Mum said I shouldn't. She said you probably feel really strange about ... well, you know.' She gave me a quick, concerned look. 'The stories that are out now, and everything. Even though they're not about *you*, exactly.'

I didn't say anything. It was true – the press were pretty much leaving Mum and me alone now, but they had all pounced on the fact that Derek Cheney of *Sole Survivor* was the mysterious Mr Y. For the last week or so, the papers had been full of screaming headlines like, **'DEREK'S SECRET PAST!** *An ex-girlfriend tells all!'*

Suddenly Uncle Derek's face was everywhere, just like mine had been, but he was always smiling, looking big and confident. And the stories were all like – ho ho, what a lad! So it didn't seem to be hurting his precious *career* after all.

Which was good, I guessed. If that's all he cared about.

Marty touched my arm. 'Do you? Feel strange about it, I mean? That he's your – well, you know. Don't talk about it unless you want to,' she added hastily.

I watched David try to bop the football off his head and miss. His friends hooted at him. 'I don't know . . . sort of, I suppose. I mean, it's like it is true and it isn't, you know?'

Marty nodded. 'Too bizarre to be real.'

'Exactly. Uncle Derek is so totally *not* a dad. Like, you know how Dad used to do the cooking, and talk to me about school and all that? Well, if it was Uncle Derek he'd just ring for a takeaway, and then talk about his series all night.'

Marty laughed, and then looked down at her nails, picking at a bit of flaking polish. 'Have you, um – talked to your dad again?'

'No.'

'Don't you think—'

'No.'

She gave me a look, like – oh, *Jules*. But the bell went then, and she didn't push it. She squeezed my arm. 'Look, we'll talk later, OK?' And she ran off to walk to class with The Weed. They walked to all their classes together now, holding hands and gazing goopily into each other's eyes.

I sighed and drifted along behind them. Suddenly I heard a burst of footsteps half-running behind me, and turned around just as Adrian caught up. He had spent break reading on his own, like he usually does. 'How's it going, Brick?'

I saw Vicki raise her eyebrows and nudge Anne, but I didn't care what Vicki thought any more. I smiled at him. 'Hi.'

He fell into step beside me and made a face, nodding at Love's Young Dream in front of us. 'Sweet, eh?'

I laughed out loud, and then clapped a hand over my mouth so Marty wouldn't hear. As if she could hear anything anyway on Planet *Lurve*.

Adrian shifted his bag on his shoulder. 'Opening night on Friday.'

'I know, I can't believe it.' I was still looking at Marty and David. I glanced at Adrian again, and suddenly realized that he was actually the only other person I could talk to about this.

'Marty thinks . . . that I should talk to my dad.'

Adrian looked at me. 'Yeah? Do it.'

'Only I don't want to. Or I do, but I just – I don't

know, I'm all confused.' I kicked a crushed-up Coke can, sending it clattering across the courtyard.

Adrian shrugged. 'Well, hey, I'll take him if *you* don't want him.'

Eh? I felt my eyebrows draw together. 'What do you mean?'

He offered me a lopsided grin. One of his shirt tails had almost escaped his trousers, and his burgundy and blue school tie had a stain on it. 'My father died in a car crash when I was two. And Mum says she doesn't ever plan to get married again, so that's it for me and dads, isn't it? So if you've got a spare one going . . .'

We had reached the science building by then, and he stepped back to let me go in ahead of me. Instead I stopped where I was, staring at him as a stream of Year Nines pushed past. His face flushed dull red. 'What? I didn't mean—'

'Adrian, listen—' I licked my lips. I didn't have a clue what to say. 'Maybe you could, I don't know, hang out with us at break sometimes? Or maybe at lunch?'

His smile could have been used to power an electric station. 'Yeah, OK.'

Mum was practically more excited about opening night than *I* was. She rang all her friends and made them promise to come and see me, droning on and on about it to them until they probably just shoved the receiver under a cushion and turned the TV on. She even read *Northern Lights*, and she hardly ever reads fiction. And *never* fantasy. She says she can't take it seriously, all that magic and other worlds stuff.

'It's fun when I can picture *you* as the heroine, though,' she grinned. 'Lyra is a wonderful character, isn't she? Only I'm not convinced by these daemons everyone has.'

'Mum! That's the best part of all.' We were sitting at the dining table, finishing up tea, a perfectly passable chicken in mushroom sauce thingee. I chewed a last bit of mushroom, swallowed. 'You can imagine the sort of daemon *you'd* have, you know? Like, I always thought I'd have a gorgeous silky white cat. With amber eyes.'

'A cat?' Mum's face creased in thought. 'No, that doesn't really suit you.'

'It doesn't? What would I have, then?' I tucked one of my legs under and propped my chin on my hand. This was like one of those personality quizzes in *Teen* magazine.

Mum tapped a polished fingernail against her mouth. 'You'd probably have . . . a magpie.'

'A *magpie?*' I shrieked. 'Thanks a lot!'

Mum looked surprised. 'Don't you like magpies? I always have. They're such beautiful birds that you expect them to be sweet and gentle, but they're not. They're tough. Resilient.'

She rose from her chair and started gathering up the dishes, piling serving bowls on top of each other with a *clink*. 'It sounds funny . . . but in a way, I'm glad that all of this happened with Ben. It let me get to know my daughter. And that's something I've learned about you, these last few months. You're strong. No-one can push you around.'

My leg unfolded as I stared at her. She smiled at me. 'I'm really proud of you, you know.' She touched my hair and went into the kitchen.

I stood up slowly, taking her plate and stacking it onto mine. A magpie.

Then I put the plates down, and went into the kitchen and hugged her. She laughed in surprise, lifting soapy hands from the sink. 'What's that for?'

'Nothing. Just – I'm proud of you, too.'

Chapter Twenty

And then, all at once it was opening night.

'Lesley, do you have to put so *much* make-up on? Nobody will even recognize me!' I stared at myself in the dressing-room mirror. My eyes looked back at me, worried. If you could even make them out in the midst of all that black eyeliner. She had turned me into a panda.

Lesley ignored me, and rubbed more beige foundation on my face and neck. 'Don't worry, it looks natural from the audience. If you *weren't* wearing any, you'd look like a ghost.'

The audience. Ice cubes slid down my spine. Almost a thousand people. All of them sitting out there, right now, waiting for the curtain to rise. Mum, Gran, Marty and her parents – *everyone*.

Well . . . not everyone. I hadn't invited Dad. In fact, I told Mum that she wasn't even to mention it to him, that I absolutely *did not* want him to come, end of story.

But had he come anyway, maybe?

Oh, God. I was going to be ill. I didn't want to do this; why had I ever thought I wanted to do this?

I was clutching my script on my lap. I took a deep breath and turned to the first page. Right, ignore the fact that there's an audience out there. Ignore the dressing room full of shrieking girls clattering about. Just be Lyra.

Oh, shut up, Pan. You always think you know what's best . . . Will you look at all this . . .

It didn't work. The words didn't mean anything, they were just words! I shoved the script onto the dressing table, rattling the lotions and tubes. 'Lesley, I don't feel well. I think I might be ill.'

Lesley *laughed*. 'You'll be fine.'

'No, I—'

She stood back and looked me over. 'Your hair should be messier, you know?' As Mrs Coulter, her own hair was swept up in a French twist, and she wore a posh red suit.

My eyes went to the mirror again. I swallowed. 'It *is* messy.'

'For real life, but not for Lyra. You're supposed to be a grungy tomboy. I'll get the hairspray.' She tripped off in her heels.

Fifteen minutes later, my hair was a red tornado that blew about my face, snarling down in wild, angry strands.

'What do you think?' asked Lesley proudly.

I think . . . I'm going to start hyperventilating and pass out.

Diane popped her head round the door. 'Ten

minutes. Scene one, take your places. And break a leg, everyone!'

'Diane, what do you think of Jules' hair?' called Lesley.

Diane came over. 'Oh yes, excellent!' she beamed. 'But we could use a bit of dirt.' She dipped her fingers into another tube, and brushed a smudge across my face. She wiped her fingers off, rubbed my shoulder. 'You look perfect. Now go on, take your place. Curtain in nine minutes.'

Nine . . . ! Minutes . . . ! My mouth turned dry. I had forgotten my lines. 'Diane, I don't feel well, I—'

Then *she* laughed. Why did everyone think being ill was *funny*? 'You'll be great. Go *on*, hurry. Get in place.'

I somehow stumbled to the wings. Adrian was already standing there in the shadows, peeking through the gap between the curtain and the wall. He turned and grinned at me. 'You should see all of these people,' he whispered. 'It's like an *ocean* of them. Want a look?'

I shook my head. Do not. Be. Ill.

He moved to my side. 'Hey, are you OK? You're not nervous, are you?'

'Maybe a bit,' I breathed.

'Me too,' he said cheerfully. 'But don't worry, Brick – you'll be great.'

My heart was still thudding sickly, but I turned and looked at him, at his round face and dark, gleaming eyes. And I wanted to say . . . Adrian, I'm sorry about your dad. You deserve a dad, and I wish you had one.

But I couldn't say it, so instead I tried to smile. 'You'll be great, too.'

From across the wings, I could see Gangly Gary, the assistant director, looking at his watch. Not yet, not yet – and then he looked over and signalled for us to get ready. I took a deep, shuddering breath. I picked up my torch and pulled at the sleeves of my tunic, adjusting them.

'You're shaking,' whispered Adrian. 'Think *ca-alm* thoughts.'

Calm, ho ho. Gary started raising the curtain. It creaked to the ceiling in a swoosh of rich red drapes.

Don't think. Just do it.

Adrian and I crept onto the darkened stage, exploring the forbidden chamber. My torch was made to look like a candle. I raised it up, showing a polished round table and wooden chairs, and tried not to let my hand tremble.

Forget the audience. Don't look at them. Just be Lyra! Oh, but I *wasn't* Lyra, I was just Jules, and I didn't know what I was supposed to be saying, or doing, and—

'Lyra, we shouldn't be here!' hissed Adrian.

And suddenly Lyra rushed through me. I actually felt her presence, like a burst of energy buoying me up. I belonged in her world; this was home.

I whirled on Adrian with a fierce, taunting whisper: 'Oh, shut up, Pan! You always think you know what's best!'

'I do not. But I'm right *this* time, and you know it! Lyra, let's go.'

I moved in a slow circle, taking everything in. 'Will you look at all this! I never thought it would be *this* grand, did you? No wonder we're not allowed in here—'

'Someone's coming!'

We scurried to the side of the stage and hid in the massive plywood wardrobe, visible to the audience but concealed from the rest of the stage. The boys who played the Master and the Butler came on.

'He's sure to be hungry when he arrives. Show him straight in.'

'Yes, Master.'

'Have you decanted the wine?'

Adrian knelt beside me, watching the action. I could hear him breathing, and I could sense the audience's entrancement. I felt like singing. Because I wasn't Lyra after all. I was Jules *being* Lyra, and that was even better. It was even better.

I allowed myself the merest of sideways glances out into the audience. Mum sat in the front row with Gran, holding a programme on her lap. Both of them looked enthralled, letting the story unfold before them. And in the second row, over to the side, sat a tall, thin man with curly hair.

Deep down, I guess I had known all along he would be there, whether he was invited or not. I had known that nothing could keep him away.

Our eyes met. Dad gave me a tiny wave. Even in the dim light, I could see that his eyes were shining and warm, supporting me.

My heart flooded with sunlight. I smiled at him.

Then I became Lyra again, gripping Adrian's arm and hissing:

'Pan, did you see that?! He poisoned Lord Asriel's wine! We have to save him!'